# CHILDREN IN REINDEER WOODS

# CHILDREN IN REINDEER WOODS

KRISTÍN
ÓMARSDÓTTIR

Translated from the Icelandic
by Lytton Smith

OPEN LETTER
LITERARY TRANSLATIONS FROM THE UNIVERSITY OF ROCHESTER

Library of Congress Cataloging-in-Publication Data:

Kristín Ómarsdóttir, 1962–
   [Hér. English]
   Children in Reindeer Woods / Kristín Ómarsdóttir ; translated from the
Icelandic by Lytton Smith. — 1st ed.
     p. cm.
   ISBN-13: 978-1-934824-35-1 (pbk. : acid-free paper)
   ISBN-10: 1-934824-35-6 (pbk. : acid-free paper)
   I. Smith, Lytton, 1982– II. Title.
   PT7511.K65H4713 2012
   839'.6934—dc23

                    2011043995

Translation of this novel was made possible thanks to the support of
Bókmenntasjóður - the Icelandic Literature Fund.

**Bókmenntasjóður**
The Icelandic Literature Fund

Printed on acid-free paper in the United States of America.
Text set in Dante.
*Design by N. J. Furl*

Open Letter is the University of Rochester's nonprofit, literary translation press:
Lattimore Hall 411, Box 270082, Rochester, NY 14627

www.openletterbooks.org

# CHILDREN IN REINDEER WOODS

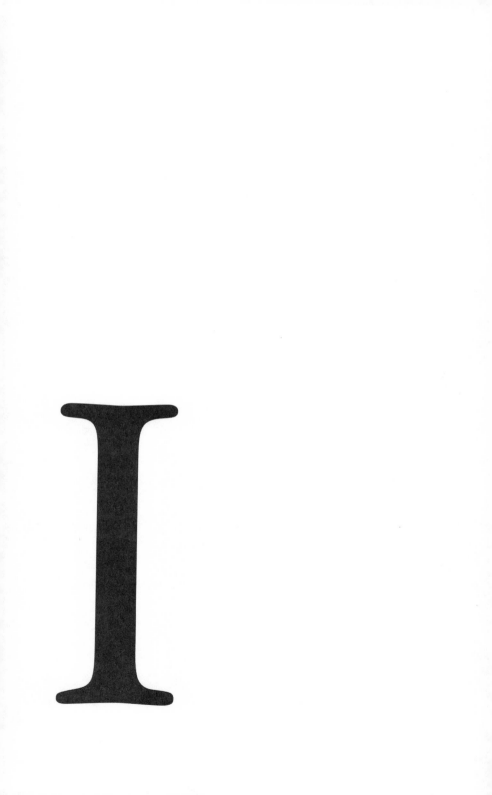

*1.* The soldiers cross the green meadow. The sun is at its height. Setting down their packs and weapons, they remove their jackets and tie them around their sturdy soldiers' waists. Three together. Three white t-shirts and three green pairs of pants approaching a farm with a two-story house that rises from a huge nest of hedges and tall trees. A cow lows in the backyard. Four, five chickens waddle about the property. A dog gets to its feet and watches the garden gate open. Four children, an older woman, and a young man head out from the house with their hands clasped behind their necks. A moment later, a woman with a red tray comes out after them. A milk bottle, a silver coffee pot, three clean glasses, three cups, a knife stuck in a thick rye loaf. Butter and freshly-boiled eggs for the soldiers. A light breeze makes its way across the yard. One of the soldiers wipes his forehead. Another watches the third, who shakes himself, brushing off goose-bumps, or a thought. On the east side, beside the gate, a pebbledash table is set into the earth. The woman with the red tray heads there. The breeze tugs at the edge of her skirt. The people stand in front of the soldiers, who shuffle their feet in the gravel. One of the soldiers shoots the woman with the tray. The milk bottle and glasses shatter. The coffee pot clatters to the ground. Blood runs from the woman's eyes as she grips the tray tightly and falls; she lies face down in the grass as if resting peacefully on a pillow, and the blood leaks across it. The youngest child runs to her but is shot on the way. The cow lows in familiar fashion. The chickens hurry over to look at the bodies. The soldier who fired lowers his weapon. The other two shoot the dog, the woman, the man, two more children. But the young girl is spared, seemingly without a thought. She lowers her arms to her sides. One soldier shoulders his weapon and takes one of the strutting chickens in his arms. "I've always wanted to hold a chicken," he confesses. The other two step cautiously inside the house, weapons raised. Army boots inside the house, bodies too. While he is examining the chicken, petting and caressing it, the girl steals under the bush near the garden gate. Into a curved tree bed. Leaves and branches cover the trees like a long grass skirt. "You smell very good, my hen. A much better scent than I expected a chicken would have. Mmm, my chick," the soldier says, pressing the tip of his nose against the hen's belly. The girl licks the salty earth, decaying leaves, mossy stones, the clods of earth. She stares out from her hiding place as the animal lover prods the chicken's belly, examines its eyes, opens its beak, and inspects the tiny tongue. No teeth. Then they call him into the house. The soldier disappears inside, the creature still in his arms. The girl pulls herself deeper into the bed on her stomach, the way reptiles move. The sun shifts. It's one o'clock.

*ii.* The trees rustled, and the curtains on the upper story were drawn by the cord. Perhaps someone could have compared the billowing of the curtains to that of a pregnant woman's dress. The cow in the backyard lowed like clockwork. The girl peered out from her hiding place. The chicken's clucking carried from the house. The chickens hadn't ever been invited inside, but this was a new era. Two more chickens strolled up to the doorstep. They finally had a chance to visit the humans' habitat. Just then the chicken inside cried out like she was about to be torn apart; there was an awful flapping of wings. The chickens hurried away. From the house, three gunshots resounded through the valley, as though the sound came from giant, well-positioned loudspeakers. One soldier dragged one of his bloody comrades across the threshold and laid him beside the other dead bodies. The cow lowed. He wiped his forehead with the back of his hand, disappeared inside and dragged out his other comrade, who was just as bloody. He wiped his forehead with the back of his hand. He went in and came back with the chicken in his arms. He moistened his handkerchief with spit and wiped splotches of blood from her feathers. He set the plump chicken down, uncoiled a yellow hose, connected it to the spigot, and turned on the faucet. There was a rustling on the ground as the cat came over to the girl, who suddenly felt her allergies prickling. The soldier set down the hose and went over to the bushes. The cat appeared from the bushes and nuzzled its head against his boots. "Here, pussy," said the soldier, taking the kitten in his arms. The girl was definitely definitely definitely about to sneeze, so she ate some soil.

**iii.** The soldier took off his t-shirt and washed his torso with the jet of water from the hose. The nozzle was an attractive orange and had three settings: a milder, more irregular jet; a sputter-spatter jet; and a strong, thundering jet. He must be using the last one. The kitty stood beside the red tray licking milk from the grass. The cow lowed from out back as though it was missing the fun, as it had on other occasions. Mooooo. The soldier sprayed water in the direction of his friend the chicken, and she danced about in the jet, her dance steps making her look like she was wearing high heels. Then he soaked the t-shirt like a rag, wiped his chest with the crumpled shirt, rinsed it, wrung it out, and hung it to dry on the narrow wooden trellis, which protected the rose bed that had been planted in front of the big French windows. On the other side, inside, by the windowsill, was the perfect spot for a portrait photograph. He picked up the hose, drank from the nozzle, and shut off the water.

The chicken followed him to the shed, where he kicked open the rusty door and got a shovel. He disappeared around a corner of the house, followed by the chicken, then reappeared and walked past the bush which stood against the garden wall—on the other side of which they had often sat in the grass to drink juice, eat cookies, and play ludo, nine men's morris, or backgammon. The chicken came back around the same corner of the house, and it took her a while, crossing the garden with smaller steps, neat chickensteps, to re-find her new friend.

Despite her restricted view, the girl could see the soldier studying part of the vegetable garden. He opened the greenhouse door, and the glass, which was too small for the frame, rattled. Beside the greenhouse grew tall, slender trees. He began to dig and shovel there. The chicken waddled around nearby. The other chickens approached, then retreated, approached again, retreated again. Done with the milk in the grass, the kitten prowled over to the girl, not interested in whether she'd like her allergies set off again; it wanted to make friends, to be affectionate towards her. Then the girl sneezed, and the kitten bounded all the way over to the soldier, who had in the meantime clambered down into the grave, which now came up to his waist. The mountain of used earth beside the greenhouse increased, and kittikins lay on the slope, watching the earth fall from the shovel onto a second mountain that was growing beside the first. The sun moved in a long arc. Tea-time came and tea-time went.

Only the soldier's head was still visible; he threw the shovel onto the bank and pulled himself up out of the grave. The girl wet herself. The soldier drank right from the nozzle of the garden hose and she saw his muscles flex. He turned the hose off, put on his t-shirt and work gloves, and dragged the body of one of his comrades into the freshly-dug grave. The body of his other comrade, too. The body of the young man, the older woman, and the woman who was still holding on to the red tray. No matter how he tried to pry the tray from her, he couldn't. The tray went in, the tray went in, it had done its service, it was ready to die. With a cigarette perched in his mouth, the soldier gathered the biggest glass shards from the grass and pitched them into the grave. Then the coffeepot, the rye bread, the butter, and the hardboiled eggs.

*iv.* The soldier gathered the dog's carcass in his arms and tossed it into the grave. He went into the house, came back with his arms full of colorful sheets, and wrapped a yellow sheet around one child's body; down it went into the grave. He wrapped another child's body in an orange sheet; down it went into the grave. The third child's body could have gone in a light blue sheet, but it got a red one instead, and down it went into the grave. The girl stared at the light blue sheet as it lay on the grass beside a yellow ball. The soldier went back to the garden gate, pushed it so hard that it rattled on its hinges, and dug about in the gravel with the toe of his boot.

He went inside and stayed there for a little while, then came back and pulled on a blue turtleneck sweater which he had gotten from his backpack. The chicken went over to him as he lit a cigarette. "Hi my hen, you sweet old lady." He blew smoke and threw the light blue sheet away, into the grave. Before the sun went down, the two mountains of earth had disappeared into the ground again. He thoroughly packed and shoveled another one-and-a-half wheelbarrows of gravel from the yard, depositing them over the fresh grave.

He sat at the pebbledash table, where the three men would have been invited to sit just after noon, had they accepted coffee and freshly-baked bread, fresh milk from the cow, and freshly boiled eggs. He lit a cigarette; there's a lot of smoking in war. The cat hopped up into his lap and lay down but got poked and vanished under the bush. The soldier stood up. The girl wet herself. He stopped in front of the bush. She saw his shoes, his fingertips. He went over to the grave. He stood there with his back to the bush, his body hunched, not upright like a soldier's. The shadows had lengthened. The girl stretched all the muscles in her body and crept out from under the bush; she chewed on her hair and snuck across the field towards the vegetable garden. Children can be invisible. She had tested it time and again. Children are more often invisible than not. The girl stood still behind the soldier. After a whole eternity, he turned around and looked in her eyes. She was wearing an off-white dress with a finely-checkered pattern; she had muddy scratched knees where stinging nettles and tree branches had snatched at her; a muddy mouth; scratched and scraped cheeks; muddy fingers; dirt teardrops under her nails; white socks and white shiny shoes; a red bow in her hair; her dress was urine-stained. There was no gun in the garden. They were all inside. She had forgotten to think about that. For a moment she had forgotten the guns. Oh, oh. They hadn't come outside, even though the bodies had, and if they did, well, she could run at once. She could run at once if they came out.

"Good evening. I am Rafael," said the man in the blue turtleneck sweater, holding out his hand.

"Good evening. I am Billie," said the girl; she curtsied and shook his hand. The chicken tripped over to them. It didn't want to let itself get separated from its new friend, which was about to happen.

V. Rafael switched on the downstairs overhead light, hunted for all the lamps he could find in the living room, the kitchen, and the hall, and lit them. He wasn't saving electricity. He turned on the light in the guest bathroom and in the office with the writing desk, the financial papers, the safe, and the French windows with roses growing on the other side of the glass. In the pantry, where there was toilet paper, candles, canned food, and empty bottles. Billie thought crossly that he wasn't following the rules of the house—taking off his outdoor shoes by the shoe rack at the front door—but she decided to keep her mouth shut for the moment. It didn't open easily unless her heart was beating fast. She took off her own shiny shoes because she made an effort to follow the adults' rules—it was easier to—and she tried to avoid stepping on the red-colored lines which had formed from congealed blood and led down the stairs from the upper level, halfway along the corridor, and all the way outside. She looked casually around for the guns. The chest under the stairs was definitely big enough for long guns. The tin key was in its usual place, in the lock. She was about to check whether the soldier had seen her inquisitive glances when he touched her shoulder and asked if she had another best dress she could put on.

"Each person only has one best dress, and this isn't mine," the girl replied.

"But this one looks so pretty."

"My best dress is prettier."

"Would you put it on, please."

"It's not Sunday. It's not my birthday. And if it's someone else's birthday, then the birthday girl is probably dead. Do the dead celebrate birthdays?" she asked.

"No, not any more. Since the number of people on earth started rapidly increasing there's no time for individual birthdays for the dead. They are all celebrated on the same day, the first of November each year."

"I did not know that," replied Billie, formally. Her mother had taught Billie to talk formally to strangers.

"News doesn't easily reach remote places like this, places where there are no trains," said the soldier.

"No planes, rather," said Billie knowingly, for although she'd traveled by plane and train to magnificent places, she'd never heard any mention of the birthday of the dead—she'd only heard of Vanity's Day, observed each year on January 14th. Her parents used to celebrate Vanity's Day, before their relationship was torn up at the roots. There were no roots. The relationship between Soffia and Abraham had grown no roots except in Billie's heart. It was foolish to plant a relationship in the heart of a child, or so she thought, she who didn't need to turn her head or move her eyes to know that the gun barrel was right by the nape of her neck. The last she'd heard, Vanity was more than two thousand years old.

"Find your best dress," Rafael commanded in a calm, resolute voice. The tone of someone who was holding a weapon. It was a deep, soft-sounding voice, quite unlike Abraham's; his was shrill. Abraham wasn't well-built and sturdy like this man; he was tall, and so thin he looked like he'd easily fall apart. How could someone who was so tall and thin hold himself upright without falling prey to the law of gravity? That's because, Abraham said in his reedy, shrill voice, I'm a puppet. A thread extends from the top of my head, but it's only visible to the puppeteers, and they live in another dimension. The same kind of thread is attached to the backs of both my hands. It doesn't take more than three threads to hold me, the puppet, up. An assortment of beings, three of them, control the threads from another planet. And so I'm hesitant, shaky, and despairing. They tug at me, each according to his own inclination.

Dad, am I a puppet, am I a puppet, Dad, am I a puppet?

No, and not mommy either, and so you're lucky and I'm also lucky because I *want* to be a puppet.

Dad, is your voice shrill because you are so tall that it stretches your vocal chords more?

No, it's actually because the puppeteer who does my voice thinks I'm in a comedy, and that was how my life was before I met mommy. How unfortunate she is to have to listen to me. And so, Billie, ssh, don't tell anyone, I am silent all day long so she can be free of my voice. My voice is not fit for such a scientific life as your mother's, though it is fit for life with my child. Yes indeedy.

When I grow up I'm going to be thin and tall and a puppet, too.

Abraham placed a finger on his daughter's lips:

Careful what you wish for, my child, for things will actually turn out that way.

Billie went up the stairs made out of thick tree logs, the gun barrel against her nape, taking care not to step in the congealed blood. It wasn't blood like when the butcher cuts lambs and chickens and their blood gushes into the grass. The earth enjoys drinking blood, he'd told her and the other kids, the owner of those very beautiful knives, that excellent mustache, and extensive paunch—a butcher has to have a paunch, or else people won't trust the meat he sells. The blood had drawn a pattern on the floor of the narrow upstairs corridor, so the girl had great difficulty finding a bloodless spot where she could get a toehold, but the infantry soldier hurried her on and she had little time to think where to step, even though she was in her socks and he in his shoes. She looked hard at his covered feet, then at her own feet, then back at his feet, then at the linoleum on the floor. Some people simply don't understand things unless they're said out loud.

On tiptoe she went into the bedroom with the red bunk, opened the red closet, and fetched her best dress. There were several dresses in the closet—Soffia firmly believed that a girl like Billie should have many beautiful dresses, and Abraham agreed: a daughter is meant to be elegant. Billie laid her best dress on the green rug. "You'll need clean underwear, socks, shoes, an undershirt, and you must have a decent sweater," the soldier said. She had a yellow sweater. With the gun barrel he browsed through the hanging dresses and folded clothes on the shelf, handed her some white socks, underwear, and the yellow sweater: "Take these and go into the bathroom."

You don't wear white socks except on Sunday, she could have said, but she kept quiet and took the clothes. A bedside lamp lay on the floor in the big bedroom beside the bathroom. Things were different from the way they were before. Before, the bedside lamp had always been on the bedside table.

Some people want to use their memories sparingly and have everything in its right place—you might run out of memory if trinkets and toys moved about too often; they should serve us, not we them. If someone constantly has to hunt for things, then they might miss the benefits of memory, which allows you to cherish wonderful moments the way a princess cherishes her earrings. Someone had told the girl this, her mother, her father, a character in a movie. She remembered who, but it wasn't worth the risk of remembering.

But this raises a problem, her dad replied, her mother, another character in a movie: if someone wastes too much of her precious memory keeping track of trinkets. The bunch of keys lives here. The bedside lamp lives on the bedside table. The address book could get long and thick, memory over-crowded. Does memory function better in chaos or order, given that order must be managed by the brain's memory cells?

So it's possible to go back and forth, debating the mechanisms inside the brain. A bedside lamp which no longer stands on a bedside table is simply a lamp.

"Take off your clothes and get in the bathtub," said Rafael, sitting on the toilet seat with his gun pointed in the girl's direction. From the look of him, he was about the same age as Marius, many, many years younger than Abraham, who refused to tally each additional year: the years make me thinner, not fatter. I don't pile them on my outsides. They whittle me like a piece of wood. So in my case it's sensible to subtract and not to add. And Billie agreed. Little by little, her daddy would disappear. She slowly undressed. Like the archaeologist unrolling bandages from the mummy—and she herself was almost literally a mummy at this point in the story.

"Do you often wet yourself?" asked the soldier.

"No."

"Does evening come early round here?"

"I don't know. I am only eleven years old."

Rafael put the gun down in the sink and mixed water in the water tank with the precision of an investigative journalist or a cocktail waiter—the right amount of hot water with the right amount of cold water, given that a child's skin is sensitive to both hot and cold. He connected the faucet to the shower head and rinsed the girl's muddy hair and body. He massaged yellow shampoo into her scalp and it rinsed off light-brown and gray. She sipped a taste of the water as it trickled down her face. He turned off the water and handed her the green olive soap: "Soap yourself," he said and sat on the toilet seat massaging his forehead and eyes. Billie soaped her arms, her wrists, her little belly, the soles of her feet, her toes who said "Hi" (invisibly, quietly); "Done," she said out loud. Then he rinsed the soap off of her body with water from the shower head, turned it off, wrapped her in a yellow towel from the shelf, dried her hair and torso, ordered her to step out of the tub, and roughly dried her legs, feet, and toes. Then he wound a towel around her hair and made a wrap on her head, the way women in Africa do. Before the war Abraham had planned to go there with Billie. The two of them. Billie and Abraham go to Africa hand in hand. Following the road with a little suitcase. They would not need much stuff. Just some clothes. Sunglasses and money. Soffia would send them money. Her dad had a beautiful brown leather wallet. Wow, how empty it had been the last time she had seen it. Wow, how beautiful it was, both when it needed money and when it was bulging.

"Those of us who are in the army are lucky: we have short hair, but other people take so much time washing and drying their hair. Isn't it hard to have hair like yours?"

She shook her head, preening, because she was a budding woman, a little chick, she'd turn heads, or so her dad said, and he seemed to know a thing or two about birds, and when he asked Soffia she'd also said yes: definitely, Billie had the makings of a beautiful woman. Someone people will talk about. Rafael fished the gun from the sink, told her to dress herself in her pretty clothes, and sat on the seat and massaged his eyes. She'd never seen a man so tired, cansado, beat, exhausted, fatigué, müte, worn-down—not in real life nor in a movie.

***vi.*** She tiptoed downstairs in her pretty rabbit-head slippers (careful not to step on the lines, careful to step not on the lines), wearing her best dress and her yellow sweater. Rafael ordered her to sit at the dinner table. On the table lay the seven-year-old boy's notebook—he would have practiced writing today, this day which had now reached its evening—and a book of maps Billie had owned since she was a year old. This book had been published long before she was born, so the borders between countries were incorrectly marked, printed in bold, contrasting colors: yellow, green, pink, red, dark blue, violet, wine red, light blue, bright green countries. Through the window in the wall which separated the living room and the kitchen, she could see Rafael moving about, busy with his kitchen work, but the rest of the wall facing Billie was covered with bookshelves, bookshelves full with the annual reports of the agricultural union, religious books, textbooks for children from six to twelve years old, books about forestry, vegetable gardening, greenhouse growing, some dictionaries, a treasury of verse, also boxes of wax colors, a set of watercolors, a red plastic chest containing toys for kids, paintbrushes, pencils, and felt-tips in a pencil case, a phone book, and a pack of candles.

Rafael's face appeared in the window: "Where did the tomatoes come from?" asked the mouth as a tomato appeared in the hand. Billie answered: "From the greenhouse." The face vanished from the window. The water in the kitchen sink went on, went off. The sounds of cooking could be heard, and at the same time as the smell of coffee reached her, the smell of eggs frying came through the window. The coffee and eggs each wanted to make its own approach to the subject, who was sitting at the dining-room table. Billie put her hand under her cheek. She was thinking. At times like this, one needed to contemplate the situation. Was she a captive now, a hostage, a prisoner of war, his booty?

She turned around in her chair and looked at the large living room window that reflected the room's electric lights, and she looked past this mirror, to where night had cleared a route through the back garden. She heard the cowbell. The same color as the darkness, the cow strolled the short stretch from the lower garden, where she spent the days, to her sleeping spot near the house. That beast of bone, meat, and muscle. Through the windowpane the girl could rush along the road and hide and hope a car would pass by. But you could count the cars that had driven along the highway this past month on the fingers of one hand. The soldier might blindly shoot bullets outside in the dark.

He set two plates on the table. On his plate were three fried eggs. On hers was a single fried egg. On each plate was a pile of baked beans, from a can, and grilled (burned, actually) tomatoes. She couldn't eat burned things. He placed two cups of steaming hot coffee on the table. Making a third trip, he brought his gun and a glass brimming with milk, which he set beside her; he wasn't about to forget she was only eleven years old.

Billie had never let coffee pass her lips—her dad said children who drank coffee stopped growing, and she planned in time to become tall and thin. Rafael affectedly balanced the gun across his thighs once he'd sat down at the table. She noticed this because she was keeping an eye on him. Why else is one born with sight? He handed her a fork and began to dig in greedily with his own, shoveling food down his throat. He didn't close his mouth between each bite, he babbled, the way Billie knew eggs make people run their mouths. But her own egg didn't manage to make her speak; she was rebelling, she wasn't going to behave by the book.

"This is a very likeable dining room, as is the living room that adjoins this room. It's homely, having a rocking chair in a room. This one is especially charming. A genuine rocking chair. Genuine rocking chairs. It's nice to have skin on the seats. I reckon it's deerskin. Are there deer in the valley?"

"No." How should Billie know.

"Wonderful to have an old-fashioned gramophone! A friend of my father had one of these gramophones when I was little. That's how things are in isolated places—in many other places they throw them away. It's been a long time since I've seen an old-fashioned wooden gramophone. Very beautiful. Wood and music. They go well together. Wood and music. It smells nice in here. Do you enjoy the jigsaw puzzles?" he asked next.

"No."

"Do you say anything other than no, Billie?"

How dare the man use her given name like that, after such a short acquaintance. Soffia used it to put emphasis on what she was saying. Abraham when he wanted Billie to hand him his glasses or something else: Billie, indulge my laziness and fetch me the watch that's on the nightstand. On the nightstand. On the nightstand. On the nightstand. On the nightstand.

"I tell the truth and nothing but the truth," Billie replied to the man's bold and unsympathetic questions. That was the best course of action in almost any situation, or so Billie felt.

"Eat your food, little girl."

"I'm not little."

"Yes, pardon me, you're big. Eleven years old. Please forgive my words, which were open to misinterpretation. When I was little I was often called 'little man.' I thought it was normal to say that."

"Then call me 'little woman.'"

"It would be impolite to call a venerable lady a 'little woman.' Eat your food," he repeated, since she had not turned to her plate.

"I'm not going to start before someone says, 'Please, go ahead.'"

"Please, go ahead," said Rafael, and he continued gobbling his food. He'd had enough with being busy, with killing people, with shoveling, with burying, with throwing away the shovel, with washing the little (but not little) girl, with preparing food, and with giving orders. Billie ate as slowly and deliberately as her father. She'd resolved to adopt his table manners as her model for this situation. Rafael scraped his plate clean and chewed the last bites until the food was no longer chewable. He drank one long gulp from the coffee cup, so that his Adam's apple rose like an ascensor, an elevator, a lift. Her dad had the strangest and ugliest Adam's apple in living memory—it had been shaped with a knife by a puppeteer on another planet. This man also had a strange and ugly Adam's apple. Perhaps he was a puppet.

*vii.* Rafael shouldered the weapon and took the crockery into the kitchen. Then he aimed the gun at the girl. "You can play for an hour before you go to bed. You'll play here."

With the toe of his army boot, he gestured to an empty spot on the living room floor. Billie got up from the table, pulled down the hem of her dress, and curtsied.

"Are you tall for your age?" he asked.

Tall like my father is, she was about to say, but stopped her motormouth dead.

"You said you were . . . eleven years old." Billie nodded her head. "Then you're tall for your age. Do you still play or not?"

"Yes."

"How does the daughter of the house spend her time?"

"I'm not the daughter of the house."

"How does a bright young thing spend her time?"

"With Barbie dolls," replied Billie, bowing because she felt she was replying to a king and kings like being replied to with bows at the end of sentences. "I am not a precocious child. I am late-developing, almost retarded, though I am not dyslexic. I believe in God, the Father, the creator of heaven and the earth."

Billie bowed. Rafael smiled without effort, and just as effortlessly the smile vanished from his face. His ordinary facial expression was in keeping with his physical strength and his deliberate movements.

"Where are the Barbie dolls?" he asked inquisitively. She pointed to the red plastic box on the bookshelf. He rummaged around in the box. "You know what? It was a pleasure to dine with you."

That's how a fully-grown man talks to a fully-grown woman, not to a girl, little or big. She stretched her back. Perhaps she'd

22

gotten big. "The pleasure was all mine," she replied, and curtsied.

"Play," he commanded, setting the red box on the floor. Billie sat down. She had heard offhand comments that eleven-year-old girls were too big for Barbie. Perhaps she was retarded. Her father and mother had said, they were always saying, the two of them together and each of them separately:

Billie dear, don't constrain your inner child.

Be a child as long as you want, even if you become the object of ridicule.

What does object of ridicule mean, Mom and Dad, what does object of ridicule mean?

When you get laughed at.

Why will I get laughed at, why will I get laughed at, Mom and Dad?

We don't know you will get laughed at, but if, if, you get laughed at, you have our word that you can be the way you want to be, so long as it doesn't hurt others. Other people's laughter is not a death sentence. You can't let others change your habits.

If she asked them whether she was retarded, they laughed like baboons. And so she took note of this, she would learn the truth for herself later. When she got bigger she would go to an institution, perhaps, and get the confirmation she currently lacked. The phone rang. Rafael, who was standing at the front door holding the cat, breathing in the evening breeze and the warm country air, turned in a half-circle and stared at the telephone. It was like he hadn't seen a phone before. Like it made a difference to stare at it. You have to answer it. Then he looked at Billie. Back at the phone. He let the cat fall from his arms and went towards the machine, which stood on a pillar in the hall. It might be Soffia. She usually rang about that time, after dinner.

The phone's ringer fell silent. The army boots continued past the girl, and the man sat down in the rocking chair.

"Does the phone ring much?" he asked, massaging his forehead.

"It sometimes rings in the morning. Sometimes in the evening. Not often."

"Who calls?"

"Someone or other."

"Do you know any names?"

She shrugged her shoulders; she couldn't possibly say, my Mom. Perhaps the man would be sorry to hear her mom wasn't dead. She dressed the Barbie dolls in new clothes, she combed their hair. The phone rang again. She acted as though the machine didn't exist. The phone went dead. Rafael's eyes closed. The cat slunk slowly across the floor, nuzzled at the rocking chair and the army boots, then jumped up onto the soldier's lap. With his eyes still closed, he made room for the animal and put a hand on its fur. The other hand grasped the weapon, which rested on his chest like a bow and violin on a sleeping fiddle player's chest. While he slept, because he snored, the playing girl took charge, and the dolls began to speak, competing to speak as though they had eaten lots of eggs, talking in soft voices:

*viii.* Ragga: I've gotten into even more trouble because I'm pregnant and going to have a child. I'll leave it on the doorstep of some rich folk. I wouldn't let anyone suffer my poverty and hardship.

Sara: I'll take the child, dear Ragga; I cannot have children because in truth I have metalbelly.

Ragga: What is metalbelly, Sara babe?

Sara: Ugh, let's not talk about it at this elegant party. Thank you for coming, my darling angel.

Ragga: Have you seen Gugga? Teddy cut off her hair and sold it.

Sara: Let's go and steal something from Teddy. Quick.

Ragga: Good idea! I likewise am dead tired of this party. It's much more entertaining to go and play outside.

Sara: I had to host this party, my darling cinnamon bun, so no one would think that I'm retarded. Sara whispers to Ragga: I am, you see, retarded.

Ragga: Me too. Don't tell anyone. Come and steal something from Teddy, Guggalugga's husband.

They arrive at bald Guggalugga's home.

Ragga: Guggalugga, you're quite the sight! You're bald.

A bald Barbie doll is added to the group.

Gugga: Don't say that, Ragga, please, be nice to me.

Ragga: It's best to speak the truth my angel, my raisin bun, I hope you're not ill, dear Gugga. Where is that guy? Where's that jerk of a guy?

The new Barbie doll, a boy-doll, who has been added to the crowd: I'm good. I'm good. As the saying goes: everything's hay in hard times. I'm good. God bless us, God bless us all. I've sinned and now I repent. All the worst things humankind has done had gathered inside me. I repented. God bless us, my child. Everything's hay—

Sara and Ragga beat Teddy to pieces.

Gugga: Girls, be nice to Teddy. It's not like you think, my hair will grow back.

Ragga: It won't grow back, you donkey, you're a doll.

They stop beating Teddy, who cries like an old crone.

Gugga: Girls, listen, please. Teddy's momma ordered him to steal my hair because she said she would disinherit him if he didn't and she gave him a lot of money for the hair. We were starving. Our stomachs howled. We would have died of hunger. Didn't you notice that we were beginning to lose weight?

Ragga: Is it better to be rich and bald?

Ragga punches Teddy.

Gugga: You're one to speak, Ragga, pregnant and about to sell some rich people your child.

Ragga: I'm not going to sell it. I'm giving it away. That's quite different. My offspring won't be bought and sold like your hair.

Sara: I shall give Gugga my hair. I'm giving Guggalugga my hair.

"Wait a moment, I need to fetch the scissors," said Billie, standing up.


**ix.** Billie wandered into the kitchen and opened the top drawer, where the scissors were kept, but there weren't any scissors there; the next-highest drawer, where they might had been put during the day's chaos, was totally empty. In the tool drawer, no tools. She searched the bookshelves and found a glue-stick, which would work well, but Rafael had gotten up from the rocking chair and was pointing the gun at her: "Sit on the floor." She went over to where the dolls waited for her, carrying the glue-stick. "You're not allowed to get up unless you need to pee, and if you need to pee ask me first and I'll go with you to the toilet." Billie bowed and sat down on the floor. Rafael sat in the rocking chair. The cat was standing in the middle of the floor, ruffled and confused, waiting to get back into its friend's lap. "What were you doing just now?"

She lifted her dolls up as an explanation: "Looking for scissors."

He closed his eyes. A few moments later he asked why she'd needed scissors.

"To cut the hair off Sara and put it on Gugga. Obviously, hair on dolls doesn't grow back."

"Hmm, knives and scissors are not playthings."

Conquering her fear, she went over to him, before the cat could leap, and handed him Sara.

"Would you cut her hair off for me, then?" she asked the soldier.

He looked at the doll, which was wearing an ivy-green sweater and beige moleskin pants.

"She has such nice hair. Do you really want to cut it?"

"She wants to give it to Gugga."

"Who is Gugga?"

"Gugga is the bald one. Teddy, her husband, cut off her hair to give it to his mom or they would have been disinherited."

He drew a Swiss army knife from his pocket and unfolded the scissors, asking how she wanted him to crop the doll's hair: cut it like a boy's or give it a Prince Valiant hairstyle.

"Crop it," replied Billie, firmly.

"Joan of Arc had a Prince Valiant hairstyle. She was a freedom fighter," Rafael explained as he cropped the hair. Then he examined the short-cropped Sara while Billie took the hair over to Gugga.

"This one is Gugga. She's bald," she said, waving Gugga; she opened the glue-stick, spread it on the bald head, and stuck the hair on. It was strong glue.

Ragga: Now we've saved your wife's head, Teddy. Isn't that good? Now you can be rich and hairy.

I love Sara, said Teddy, I have fallen in love with her, my heart bursts in my breast from my desire for her—"Hey Mr. Man, can I have Sara?"

Rafael came over, bringing the girl Sara, and knelt down, examining the collection of dolls on the floor with one hand— he was using the other hand to hold the gun. Billie felt the burning scent of aftershave, the smell of tobacco, the smell of earth and of sunshine. Cat hair on his blue turtleneck sweater. Dark stains on his trousers. What was it like to wear army boots in a living room?

Teddy: I love you more than my own christening-party, my own wife, my mother and father, more than the omnipotence, than fortune itself, Sara babe: will you marry me, Sara babe?

Sara: No, I'd never marry a man who couldn't risk living on the verge of starvation but instead slices off his own wife's hair to give to his mother, shame on you Teddyman.

Sara stamps her foot and runs off, crying.

Teddy: I love you, Sara, I will never be able to love anyone else in the world, Sarababe.

Sara: I am not your babe, I'm no one's babe.

Ragga: Sara, don't go, wait for me.

Ragga to Teddy: Sara has never loved anyone but you, she told me long ago, before you married Guggalugga.

Teddy: O poor, wretched me, I'll kill myself tonight, my heart has been mashed like a potato.

They all run after Sara.

Teddy attacks Gugga: You scarecrow, you scarecrow, I hate you, I hate you, you've disgraced and destroyed my life because I can never love anyone but Sara who cut off her hair so you could have beautiful hair.

Gugga: Don't be mad at me, it's not my fault that I was hairless, was it, you shameful man?

Sara: You oughtn't talk in such a way to your wife, Teddy, or things will deteriorate.

Sara is about to jump off a steep mountain.

Ragga: Sara, don't do it, please, remember your child in my stomach, our child in my stomach.

Sara: I've nothing left to live for, people are evil, the man I loved has disappointed me, I say farewell, dear Ragga, you can have all my clothes and please be nice to Gugga, be nice to Gugga—

Sara jumps off the mountain. Ragga begins to weep: I will kill Teddy's mother. She destroyed everything and now my child will forever be an orphan.

Gugga cries quietly.

Teddy runs to the mountainside and throws himself down too, ooof, they're both dead. Billie draws deep, gasping breaths even though she herself hasn't run anywhere. Just the four dolls. Two of them dead.


**X.** "Now it's time for a little girl to go to bed," said the thick mouth on the large face; it was as close to her as her own reflection in the children's bathroom mirror. His pocked cheeks reminded her of the surface of pudding, with downy hair on the earlobes. Her dad was never clean-shaved like this, but often rough with little red shaving cuts.

"A big girl," she corrected him. "I am the last to go to bed because I'm the oldest. I often stay up with the grown-ups. I look after the little kids, I'm responsible for them in the evenings."

She held herself up jauntily and spoke as though no one had died just after noon. Without warning, he picked the girl up from the floor and held her up in the air. Since she'd stopped being little, long ago, no one had held her. Her dad was too thin. This person had a muscly, incredibly stout neck, as broad as his head. The cat hair on the sweater tickled her nose—"God bless you," said her porter. What god? He set her in the lower bunk, right where she usually slept. Strange. He looked for her night-things in the closet and set them beside her. Blue pajama bottoms. A top with pictures of different colored birthday presents wrapped with beautiful, colorful ties and bows. As he studied the window fastenings, she wondered whether she should ask him for her own night-things instead. The window could open, but it was impossible for a child to get through the narrow gap without, or even with, a screwdriver. He loosened the string which was fastened to the handle under the windowsill with a fisherman's knot and set the tangle on the ledge. He drew the curtains, which featured a crowd of villains with masks over their eyes and gloves on their hands, villains holding bright, illuminated flashlights up in the air. He lit the nightlight, the shade of which had pictures of angels with planets in their arms; he turned off the ceiling light, went out, and came back. By that time Billie had gotten ready for bed. He asked why she didn't cover herself with the comforter. She didn't reply, so he covered her with the comforter, turned off the light on the bedside table, and started to shut the door.

"I can't sleep with the door shut."

He left it open a crack, which turned into a thin border of light once the hallway ceiling bulb was switched on. Rafael went to the upstairs bedroom. He moved the furniture, something bounced down the stairs, he dragged a mattress across the floor, he ran water in the bathroom sink, he flushed the toilet and flushed the toilet again, maybe to watch the flow. Flushed the toilet. Flushed the toilet. He opened a drawer, the closet doors. Something was lifted up and set down on the floor, possibly a suitcase. The coat hangers that held the clothes in the hallway closet were moved back and forth on their rail. Then the vacuum cleaner was turned on, and the girl fell asleep amid the noise. During the night she was awakened by someone else's snoring; she fell asleep again, woke and waited for the gray-black shadows to turn themselves into images. On the floor in front of her bunk was a mattress. Rafael was lying on it under a blanket. The gun lay on the floor on the far side of the mattress. The cat lay at Rafael's feet. Billie closed her eyes.

Billie Billie Billie
My girl with the dreamy eyes
Her stubborn dreamy eyes which can't be free
Until father lulls you to sleep

Billie Billie Billie
My girl with the dreamy eyes
Her stubborn dreamy eyes which can't be free
Until mother lulls you to sleep

Billie Billie Billie

My girl with the dreamy eyes

Her stubborn dreamy eyes which can't be free

Until Marius lulls you to sleep


*xi.* Without waking the cat, Rafael got up, wearing a man's nightgown and white army socks, opened the curtains, looked outside, reached for the gun, crept out, and pulled the door quietly closed after him. She heard him urinating. The water running in the sink. Perhaps he was washing himself in a military fashion. A creaking from the stairs, the first steps of a new day, the brittle wood shifting after the cool nighttime breeze and a few hours' lack of use. When should she get up? Now, right away, soon, never? Billie sneezed. She rubbed sleep from her eyes, the way people do in movies, and walked over the mattress. Perhaps the soldier thought he was a kid, sleeping like that on the floor in the children's bedroom.

In the corridor she encountered the familiar smell of cleaning: eucalyptus and coconut. The bloodstains had vanished from the hallway and from the wall in the master bedroom. Barefoot, she tripped down the scrubbed clean steps of the stairs and snuck her feet into her rabbit slippers, which were waiting for her on the shoe rack. Rafael was standing by the kitchen stove in blue farmer's pants and a white shirt, his bare feet in blue flip flops, frying bread he'd dipped in beaten eggs. Coffee dripped from an orange funnel down into a wine-red thermos. The washing machine and dishwasher pumped water into themselves. Tally-ho.

"Early riser," he said when she appeared with the doll Gugga in her arms.

"I'm both a morning rooster and a night raven," Billie said proudly, hreykin, stolz, orgullosa.

"I'm a sleepyhead by nature. That's a good reason for a young man to join the army. It told me one thing: join the army, and they'll teach you to get on your feet." He turned the bread over in the pan, *blam*. "If I'd been able to wake up on my own or with the help of an alarm clock, I'd have studied to be a veterinarian. But out in the country a man can find a natural alarm clock. The rooster."

He moved the bread from pan to plate and moistened more slices of bread in the egg mixture.

"This is the first time I've been to the country. No one ever told me that perhaps I could become a farmer. Not that I needed other people to sort out my dreams—I wanted to be a vet. What do you want to be when you grow up?"

"An astronomer," said Billie, sitting down at the kitchen table. Her slippers fell off her feet. The window at the kitchen table showed the garden in front of the house. The soldier's pants were hanging on the clothesline. On the pebbledash table his army boots, shiny and polished, stood on some newspaper. The sun had not yet started making its way across the sky.

"Tell me, little girl . . ."

"Big," she corrected, placing her hand sleepily under her chin.

"Who is lying out there in the garden? Your siblings?"

Billie shook her head.

"Your parents?"

She shook her head.

"Do you know them?"

"Yes."

He set two pairs of cutlery and two plates of eggy bread on the table, poured coffee into cups, milk into a glass, said, "Please, go ahead," and sat down. Billie handled her cutlery. She knew how to eat with her hands (God's cutlery), with only a fork, with both knife and fork, and with chopsticks.

All astronomers eat with either chopsticks or with a knife and fork, but never with only a fork. In days gone by, the astronomers had made an agreement: in order to defend themselves against the prejudices of others, they would conduct themselves in a particular way, by means of an agreed-upon style of their own, certain formal manners and courtesies, her mother explained one day, holding her fork in her left hand, her knife in her right hand, giving Billie a demonstration.

I don't understand, Mom—

No. I am practicing being eloquent myself—at the same time as I'm talking to you the way grown-ups do, so that you get training in the grown-up art of conversation. That way you'll be at home at elegant parties in the future. Your dad can't teach you the art of conversation because he doesn't know it. You see, Billie, watch what I'm doing with my knife and fork. You need to know that to be an astronomer, babe.

Mom, Mom, I can't wait to become big. Will I be as beautiful as you?

Much much much more beautiful, darling chick.

Rafael ate his eggy bread like an astronomer. Perhaps he'd received training in the army to defend himself against the prevailing prejudices. A protocol for manners. Her dad couldn't use a knife with a fork, only either a fork or chopsticks, because otherwise it would be fiendishly hard if puppeteer one was conducting the fork and puppeteer two the knife: one and two never wanted the same thing, and it was best to let one or the other of them handle the eating. Rafael and Billie each cut bites of their eggy bread slices; she tried to stab the bites into her mouth at the same time as him, but he suddenly looked out the window like a wise man in a movie and asked if she wanted tomato ketchup or syrup with the bread. She asked for both and he hunted for both in the fridge. Good. Excellent service.

"Where are your parents?" he asked once he had sat back down at the kitchen table.

"I don't know. Maybe they're dead."

"Has it been a long time since you were last with them?"

"Three-and-a-half months. That's when I came here."

"Tell me about the people in the grave. What are they called?"

"Marius, Inga, and Jenny. They set up a nursery that invited kids to come and stay here. Lisa, Frank, and Karl were the kids' names."

"Does anyone else live here?"

"Isaac, sometimes."

"Who is Isaac? Where is he now?"

"A shepherd. Somewhere up in the mountains with the sheep and lambs that were born in the spring. The ones that weren't killed."

"Were the lambs killed?"

"The butcher killed them. They were sold to restaurants."

"Does anyone else live here?"

"No"

"Think hard."

"I did."

"Aren't you forgetting someone?"

"No."

"Marius, Inga, Jenny, Lisa, Frank, Karl, Isaac, and Billie. Four men and four women."

"I'm not a woman. Lisa isn't either."

Rafael sipped from his coffee and dried his mouth on a paper napkin, as though his mouth was a stamp and the paper towel was a letter. Billie did the same. Dried her mouth as if it was a stamp and the paper napkin an important document. What fun it was to kiss a paper napkin.

"Who owns the orange car in the garage?"

There was no need to be solemn, but one certainly ought to be formal during interrogations. The minimum respect for the rules in order to be taken seriously.

"I don't know."

"It's very serviceable, I know that much, you're not hiding anything from me."

"I don't know whose it is," she said, firm as a rock and a little sharply. She knew how things were, this girl.

"Who drove the car?"

"Marius, Inga, Jenny . . . they all drive it."

"Where did they drive it?"

"One time Inga drove the car to Forever Valley. Marius drove down into this valley to pray."

"To pray?"

"It's good to pray down by the ruins."

"And Jenny?"

"Jenny took us kids on a trip down to the lake. For a picnic."

"What car were you in when you came here in the spring?"

"All of us kids came in a minibus."

"Who drove the bus?"

"A bus driver."

"There was no one else in the bus but the bus driver and you kids?"

"Isaac."

"Isaac?"

From the movies she knew the trick interrogators have of repeating what someone has said back to them so that they might let something slip in the next breath.

"Isaac."

"What was Isaac doing?"

"Going to lead the herd, of course. What a shepherd does in spring, goes up the mountain with the herd and travels with it. He was also attending the lambs' birthing, so he could know them from the first day. That's important for a shepherd. Isaac said so."

"The lambs' birthing," Rafael repeated, and he fell silent. The questions trailed off just at the point when she was beginning to enjoy answering them. If this was a game, she clearly hadn't lost, but it was boring to play with a man who stopped mid-turn, when it suited him, even though she wasn't done.

"My dad's a puppet," she said.

"What's that?"

"A puppeteer on another planet controls his movements and actions."

"Are these puppeteers our enemies? Enemies of the army?"

"They don't interfere in the war. They only interfere with Dad. They hold on to him using an invisible thread through his head and the backs of his hands. But if it weren't for this, he wouldn't be able to hold himself upright, resisting the law of gravity, since he is too tall and thin. One of the puppeteers tells him to go left. At the same moment another puppeteer says he should go right. That's not easy. At the same moment a third tells him to go home and sleep. One tells him to wake up. One tells him to drink. Another tells him to read. One loves Mom. One doesn't love Mom, although he pretends to."

"Hmm. Unusual," said Rafael.

"They might be ready to raise him up at this very second. Who knows."

"What?"

"The puppeteers, raise Dad up. He expects they are going to raise him up when they feel he's stayed on earth long enough."

"Mmm. And your Mom? Is she a puppet?"

"No. Maybe she's dead."

Billie wanted Rafael to look her in the eyes—she'd prepared exactly the right facial expression—but he didn't: he poured the rest of the coffee into his cup and poured the coffee from the cup into himself. Better if he just poured it directly into himself from the thermos rather than using all those intermediary steps.

"Good coffee," he commended himself, lit a cigarette, opened the outside door, and greeted the chickens who were waiting by the doorstep and who rejoiced at his appearance on this new day.

"Good day, my dear, dear hens," he said, taking one of them in his arms and going out to the garden. The others followed in his footsteps. The gun lay on the fridge. Should the girl keep eating her food? She reached out for the green felt-tip pen, which was in a basket on the kitchen table, and began to color the white tabletop without thinking—but there were a lot of other things to think about. She colored a green swath about the size

38

of two big pencil cases, so thoroughly it wasn't possible to see the white beneath.

*xii.* Flip flops weren't something she'd seen on the farm before, nor had she ever seen a soldier's bare feet, not in real life and not in the movies. She stopped coloring the table when Rafael came in from the garden and took off the flip flops in the entryway; she poked inattentively at the crocheted tablecloth under the basket and wondered, with good reason, if this was a notable event in her life: I saw a soldier's toes when I was little, and they weren't that different than other people's toes. Not unlike my father's toes. No different than my mother's toes. She would be able to tell the story later on. The feline pursued Rafael, and after it came two, three chickens—he was popular—who peeked into the living room, observing the furnishings with a speculative look.

"I fed the chickens and got the freshly-laid eggs," he said proudly, showing Billie his open hand. Three eggs lay there. "That's something I've never done before in all my life. I'm a born farmer." Then he noticed the gun up on the fridge, put the new eggs in a yellow-colored bowl, took the weapon, and pointed it at Billie. "Kindly—please, go ahead—head up and get dressed, clean your teeth, then come back down once you've finished."

Billie slipped down from her chair, "Straight back," he commanded, "straight back." She tugged the doll Gugga with her, and lugged her body about the way kids do when they feel totally lazy, without any interest in exerting themselves.

"Should I wear my best clothes like yesterday?"

"Yes."

"Is it Sunday?"

"No, Tuesday," said the boss, raising the gun in the air as she plodded up the stairs. When she came back down he was sitting at the kitchen table with the cat in his lap, smoking, writing in a black book, and massaging his forehead. The gun lay on the crocheted tablecloth. The green square on the table was still green. Billie handed him a hairbrush and a red hairband. He prodded the cat in the rump, and she leapt, miffed, down to the floor. Rafael stuck the hairband between his lips the way her mom and dad did and Marius did too. Then he combed her hair lock by lock, pulled the hair up, retrieved the elasticated band, and drew it around the base of the ponytail, high on her nape.

"There," he said. Billie tossed her ponytail and thanked him. She was wearing patent leather shoes with red bows, yellow socks with green tassels, and a yellow dress with red buttons.

"You are very, very elegant. I should button my top button and tie a red bow around it. Is there a red bow anywhere in this house?"

She pulled open the top kitchen drawer. Billie was a girl who loved to rummage in drawers.

"Stop," said Rafael, aiming the gun at her, "from now on you don't touch the kitchen drawers or cabinets."

She couldn't read the expression in his eyes, but at least he would not be able to read fear in hers—despite the gun, she was not scared one bit.

"I was just looking for a red bow," she said, her voice revealing little or no fear, even though she had snuck a smoker's pipe knife in her hand, the more-or-less infant knife in the knife family, and she raised the knife up in the air. Rafael smiled at first, before he apprehended the seriousness of the situation, then the smile froze on his face. Billie leaped forward, aiming the knife where his heart was. He collapsed away from her. The chair slammed onto the ground and the gun shot across the floor. The knife came down in his chest but there was no blood. The cat got up from her heap, her curiosity sparked. The chickens hurried away. No thanks. They didn't care for these dramatics. The girl sat down on top of the soldier and made a second attempt to kill him, but he disarmed her. He held her firmly around her wrist and studied the pipe knife. Then he unburdened himself of the girl-pile and climbed to his feet.

"Did you mean to kill me?"

She didn't answer.

"You aimed for my heart."

"You aimed the gun at me."

He offered her the pipe knife: "Stab me where you want."

She stuck the knife in his stomach. This guy didn't bleed.

"Yes, well, now playtime's over," he said. He disarmed her without a struggle and put the knife away in a drawer at the same moment as the phone rang. He looked at the phone. It is not enough to just look at the phone, you also have to answer it, which was not likely to happen. Rafael watched as the phone finished ringing, buttoned his shirt to the neck (it lacked a bow but that would have to do), and took Billie's hand: "Be so kind as to show me the garden, my little imp of a girl."


*xiii.* "There are the apple trees and there are the pear trees and there are the plum trees," said Billie, pointing out the apple trees and pear trees and plum trees; she wasn't in the mood to point out the orange trees, "but there away from the center and all by itself is a lemon tree, as you can see. Those lemons weren't picked in spring, they're spare lemons, good for popping out into the garden when you need them for salad. Do you see the fountain by the lemon trees? You can turn on the water and then the boy pees into the pond. Three orange goldfish live in the pond; they're called Isaac, Albert, and Maria. They want to be together forever. They are best friends. Do you want to see them?"

She led the man to the fountain behind the house. There were two white-lacquered chairs made out of thick wood, so heavy that the kids couldn't lift them. The grass grew wild around the chairs' feet. It was in these chairs, by the fountain, that the grown-ups enjoyed sitting and talking together. About their feelings. The way two men once had in the moonlight, dressed in t-shirts and blue jeans, one lighting cigarettes at regular intervals, all the better to keep the tobacco producers of the world working. Talking about politics: the struggle to feed and clothe all mankind. About religion: does God exist, does God not exist. About science: is the universe a delusion, is there a justice independent of energy, does evolution take place, does evolution not take place, are there rules, is there chaos. She had noticed seriousness, anxiety, carelessness, quick tempers, heart-rending joy in the faces of the seated people. They peered into the pond. At the three orange fish.

"Why are they called Isaac, Albert, and Maria?"

"Isaac is called Isaac after the shepherd. Albert is called Albert after Inga and Jenny's father, Marius's grandfather. Maria is called Maria after a friend of Marius."

"Who is Maria?"

"She lived in the city where Marius lived before he moved here."

"When did Marius move here?"

"When he'd had enough of ballet. He was a ballet dancer who set his dance shoes back on the shelf."

"And moved here?"

"Not immediately. Before that he lived alone in a little house on the edge of the city. In the house opposite the King of Rock and Roll. So he moved here."

"The King of Rock and Roll?"

"Yes. He was very lonely. Always down in the basement playing billiards with his friend. When Marius saw that, he realized that you shouldn't live for yourself but for other people. Marius wanted to look after animals and other people's children. He waited, hoping that Maria would return to him, but she never came. A man cannot wait forever. 365 days is an acceptable length of time for a lover to wait, but once the earth returns to the same place it was when the waiting began, it's over, the waiting ends. Marius waited 366 days because it was a leap year."

"Show me more," the soldier asked, and the girl led him to the vegetable garden.

"The potatoes grow here. The onions grow there. The carrots grow there. The cabbage grows there. The spinach grows there. The strawberries grow there. This is a good spot to lie down if you don't want to be found because no one in the house can see you here. Here's the cow. She's not called anything. Some want to call her Flora, but I think that's an ugly name, like mucking out the floor or something."

"Do you know how to milk her?"

"No. Come on."

"No, hold on, I want to try to milk the cow, I've never milked a cow."

He pulled in one direction, she pulled in another, almost like two of the puppets having a tug of war over her dad. She got the upper hand, dragged him into the greenhouse and showed him the roses, the tomato plants, the experimental fruits, and the seasonal herbs. They went back outside and then into the hen house.

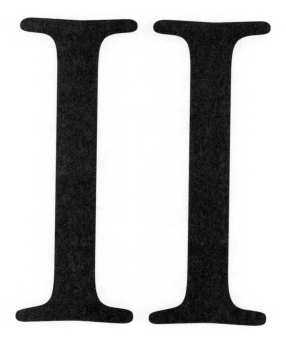

*xiv.* Billie sketched hopscotch in white chalk on the pavement in front of the house. Dressed like a farmer, Rafael headed across the lawn with a pail, and the chicken straggled in his footprints, pecking in the grass. Further off on the property, the cat was chasing birds. The sun shone, but the girl didn't squint because she was in the shade of the house, wearing jeans and a denim jacket, with a pigtail and a pink band in her hair. She was wearing pale pink canvas shoes and yellow socks. She threw a green stone into a chalk box then hopped into the box on one foot and picked up the stone. Rafael came around the other side of the house with a full pail of fresh milk from the teats.

"She's very big, that cow," he said. "I would never have believed before what a handful such animals are, so big and heavy and bulky. In pictures they aren't that big—and they never eat anything but grass. A huge flock that only eats grass. That's obviously been a ploy to lobby for meat eating. Conspiracies and lobbying by farmers and butchers. One should get sustenance from grass alone, according to that logic."

Barefoot, he went inside, set the pail on the kitchen table, announced he was tired, he had such a horrible headache that he was going to go and lie down. He lay down on the mattress in the children's bedroom, the gun on the floor beside the mattress, and immediately fell asleep. Billie watched him from the top steps of the staircase, having little else to do with her time. If not this, then it would have to be hopscotch, skipping rope, music she'd collected and which she would listen to from time to time with her ear buds in her ears, or the Barbie dolls, who were now mostly bald and dead. She dozed right there on the steps. The outside door was wide open. A few chickens peeked in for a visit. The smell of sleep had reached them, giving them courage, courage enough to push further into the peoples' living quarters, to stroll around the living room. To peer at the red chest with the Barbie dolls and the brand new paper dolls which the soldier had cut out for the girl, cackling among themselves in a way humans cannot comprehend—and unexpectedly (or not) the gramophone's turntable began to turn as they populated the room. It played an old tune, a fun song to dance to. But the chickens shook their heads. They didn't like the look of things; they pecked at the loudspeaker. The turntable's arm rose. It wasn't going to play for deaf or unfriendly ears.

The chickens waddled outside and across the lawn, home to their hen house, pecking often and cackling. The girl came back to reality on the top step of the stairs, crawled over the floor, and lay down on the mattress beside Rafael. In his sleep he made room for her, and her eyes closed. Never has anyone known such broad shoulders, such a big and strong back, such infinitely thick arms. This person wouldn't need a string from another planet to hold him upright.


**XV.** She woke in the fetal position, which her parents had praised and commended, saying it could save one's life. If someone vomited in their sleep, they wouldn't suffocate if they were in the fetal position, and, moreover, the fetal position soothed stomachaches and stopped internal bleeding. Once there was a young guy who was prone to vomiting copious amounts of blood at night. He never slept in anything but the fetal position. At night, he would stand over the sink at intervals, alone, and vomit. The windows were dark. The bath tiles cold. His toes and soles were ready for fun, but his stomach and organs were reluctant.

"Hi Billie," Rafael said, sitting up and staring at the girl who is lying on his mattress.

"Hi soldier. How is your headache?"

"I am a little better"—he dried the blood that was running from his nose on to his nightgown—"though I have a nosebleed. Perhaps it's caused by the strain to my head. I've had migraines for the last few years. My mother had migraines."

Then he retrieved the gun from the floor, stood up, and got his clothes from the back of the chair. She gaped at his squeaky-clean soles.

"Is she dead?"

"No, but the migraines are gone. They often leave people. Like childhood allergies," he replied and wandered off. "Damn, what the devil, the chickens have crapped over everything!" he shouted, stopping on the stairs in his bare feet and nightgown, his clothes and the gun in his arms. "Wretches, demons, plague-bearers. Those bastards. Shit imps!"

The floors in the hall and the living room were soiled with chicken mess. Billie sat down briefly on the top step and watched as Rafael leaped across the floor on his toes and grabbed the army boots, which were standing, polished and shiny, on the porch. He put the boots on and spread yellowish-brown soap over the floor from a bottle.

"Were they mocking us?"

"I don't know," replied Billie, who would be picking her nose if cleanliness wasn't the topic of conversation.

"They have the whole house and garden to shit in, and yet they come here, to us. We don't head over to their place to do our business."

"There's no need to take it personally."

She hadn't talked like that before, and it felt funny in her mouth; her ears had heard that sentence said before, on many different occasions.

"Of course I don't take it personally."

"Chickens are chickens."

"They might be emissaries from another planet. A farmer shouldn't need to clean up chicken crap in his own home," he said, pouring boiling hot water into the pail, snatching a brush and a rag, and beginning to scour the floor. Stop grumbling, she almost said, but because she felt a funny flutter in her body, she disappeared into the bedroom, where she sat on the orange chest of drawers and waited for this odd feeling to pass. She bit her lip and inner cheek until she broke the skin, drawing blood. When the pain started she felt a little better. The growing numbness that tingled under her skin would vanish if she bit herself hard enough.

She opened the curtains. They hadn't been opened yet, even though it was the middle of the afternoon and the sun had vanished behind the clouds. Rafael yelled: "Ah!" Perhaps he'd stubbed his toe on the table, poor man, with his short fuse. She'd seen people in movies with short fuses screaming for the smallest reason. It didn't kindle her interest.

Instead, she decide to make the mattress-bed. She rolled the grey army blanket inside the bedsheet, carefully set the multi-colored, crocheted bedspread down on the roll, and then made her own bed. Now the bedroom was nice. What fun it was being in a nice bedroom. Rafael would be glad to know she was someone who tidied things, not like the chickens. She opened the window, the way you do when you're cleaning. Her mother always opened the window right after she opened her eyes, both movements equally automatic, opening her eyes, opening the window, opening the window, opening her eyes. She sat back up on the orange chest of drawers, closed her eyes, and prayed: Dear God, let me be good. Then she squeezed her eyes shut again and grasped the chest of drawers tight as her body began to swim away into the measureless regions of outer space. To avoid disappearing there, she opened her eyes. The bedroom was still here. A mechanical snoring sound reached her ears, and it quickly turned into the sound of an airplane—that definitely kindled her interest. It meant she didn't have time to tidy the bedroom: the unknown was calling.

As she stood in the front doorway, putting on her pink canvas shoes, she noticed, even though the noise of the airplane was driving her crazy, a chicken hanging from a pole, string around its neck. Dressed in his army gear from head to toe, Rafael was standing further up the yard, watching through military-green binoculars. The airplane buzzed over the valley, spitting out white smoke. Billie pulled on Rafael's pants' leg: "Why have you hung the chicken? Why did you hang the chicken, why have you hung the chicken, why did you hang the chicken? Answer me, fella. Executioner, more like! You didn't announce the execution, not once. An execution under the cover of silence, under cover of silence, under cover of silence. What kind of doomsday executioner are you, you mean fella? Why did you hang the chicken, fella?"

"Don't tug at my pants, miss," he ordered, but she hit her fists against his body and bit him in the thigh. A good bite. On his thick, muscled thigh. He hooked his fingers around the girl's chin and asked if she'd gone mad. The saliva ran from her mouth. He shoved her away before the saliva could find its way onto his clothes; her face smashed into the grass, but she didn't hurt herself. She could, though, have cracked her chin or broken her nose; it's happened to others, like, for example, boxing champs. She rubbed her chin in the grass and looked up. Rafael lowered the binoculars:

"That's our plane. Those are our men."

He waved his arms. Like dancing with the airplane, which made another pass over the valley and dived over the meadows and moors east of the farm. Someone in a parachute jumped from its belly, followed by a black case hanging from a parachute. Rafael stretched, craned. "It's a crying shame not to have a dog," he mused.

The airplane accelerated, rose, and vanished back towards

the south-east as Rafael stood straight as an arrow, his hand on his forehead, a real soldier's greeting; the low-ranking soldier had decided to obey his commands today. Perhaps his dreams of farming were over, forgotten. When someone is young, they change dreams like they change their socks; a movie said so. It's worse as one gets older, because then you get trapped in one of the many dreams, repeating yourself, repeating yourself, repeating yourself, people freeze and cannot make themselves stir. People constantly change their clothes when they're young. Always wears the same clothes when they have grown old.

The plane disappeared from view, and Rafael snapped his heels together, brought his hands down by his sides, and shouted over the noise, his words echoing: "Sir, yes sir." He snapped his heels together again, repositioned the machine gun that was hanging from his shoulder, and marched, straight as an arrow, out of the garden.

*xvi.* This determined behavior, and his soldierly mood, piqued Billie's curiosity and appealed to her sense of humor; it changed everything. The allure of the unknown enchanted her out of the garden and after the soldier; he didn't prevent her from following him, even though she wasn't a dog or a full-sized person. She skipped over the tussocks, so agile in the world's best canvas shoes; she was waiting for him to say: Wow, how great those sneakers are! I've never seen such good sneakers. You can really jump in them. They must have magical powers! Yes, mom gave me them.

She jumped over a stream. Look, man, how good my sneakers are. Have you ever seen such skipping shoes? Mom gave them to me. I can jump like a spring-man, a spring-man, a spring-man.

He strode over the same stream, but his movements weren't small, or soft; he was as stiff as a wooden man. "A real shame not to have a dog, they can smell everything." Grumbling and mourning and missing a dog and hanging the chicken, all within the space of an hour.

Like the way a tin soldier's body always assumes the correct posture whenever the army's general is around, this man stretched himself upright whenever the potholed landscape forced him to stoop. It wasn't easy to march over holes and tussocks.

They came down into a hollow, and there was a man sitting next to a parachute, a checked guitar case, and a military-green backpack. He was dressed in a black leather jacket with black fur on the collar and army pants; he was massaging one of his feet, which was shoe- and sock-less. He grinned from ear to ear at the approaching visitors. But who was the visitor and who was the host? Rafael stilled himself, moving his hand to his forehead.

"Good day, sir," he said in a loud voice. The wind and being outside made it necessary for him to really use his voice.

"Good day, sir. Good day, señorita," the man answered, freeing himself from the baseline which connected him to the parachute.

"Good day, man-in-a-parachute," replied Billie, curtseying.

"It's good that you've come. I hurt myself in the fall," he said, pointing at his foot.

Rafael placed his hand back on his forehead: "Rafael here, member C in infantry division regiment B-3, OP-17."

"Peter here, sent to scout this area and bring information to infantry division regiment B-3."

"You're in the right place," answered Rafael, snapping his heels together.

"And who is the girl, if I might ask?"

Rafael set his hand on his forehead.

"She is called Billie, and she lives in the only farm in the valley. Children in Reindeer Woods. It's a sort of temporary home for children. The people went camping, according to the girl's story, left her behind alone at the farm. They haven't come back. As far I can work out, she's been orphaned," said Rafael, returning his arm to his side once he'd finished talking.

"A home for children. Children in Reindeer Woods," Peter aped Rafael, as if fixing the words in his memory. "A little Cinderella. Hmm. Remarkable. Left in the home for children when people went camping. An interesting series of events. Little Cinderella."

"Not so little, actually rather big for her age," corrected Rafael.

The parachutist squinted his eyes, even though clouds were covering the sun.

"Is this Reindeer Woods?"

"It's wherever you want it to be," answered Billie, stepping into the conversation with a curtsey.

Peter laughed. He had beautiful teeth. A mouth like a shark.

"A wonderful answer. I asked out of complete ignorance—we don't know a single place name in these parts. It's truly a hidden grove. It would be good to fill the empty space on the map with at least one word, Reindeer Woods," he looked around him, "but there are no woods?"

"Well, up the slope of the mountains," said Rafael, pointing in the direction of the mountains.

"The slope of the mountain," repeated Peter, and he looked around harder; perhaps he was squinting because he was near-sighted. "Fine and dandy. I can't get to my feet without the gentleman's help."

Rafael extended Peter a helping hand.

"The crate is someplace over there," said Peter, very cautiously putting his weight on his foot. "It contains provisions for infantry regiment division B-3. I expect the team are quite lunch-less after all this time."

Billie curtsied to him:

"Would sir like me to carry his shoe and guitar case?"

"With pleasure," answered the parachutist, smiling at Billie like no one ever had. The first smile. It happened in this hollow. The parachute lay on the grass like a bridal veil, and Billie was sure that the earth would be lonely, the parachute too, if she separated them—but it would be fun to own a parachute. She would be able to boast some time later: Yes, it's true, I am indeed the esteemed owner of a parachute. That said, she would never tolerate bragging.

They started walking, following his directions to the black case's likely landing place. Rafael went at the head of the group, with an air about him which was either modesty or anger. Peter followed him, stepping gingerly every other step.

"I always land in trouble when I parachute jump, without exception. The most accident-prone parachutist in the army has arrived in Reindeer Woods. My last jump ended up in stinging nettles. The time before that I fell through a thatched roof into a tub of water. Which was a good thing, because the child who was bathing in the tub had gotten out to chase a cat just after pooping in the water. Wasn't it better that I landed in poop than crushed a child? That was good luck out of bad luck. That's what I said. And more than that: the child's mother and I drank tea together that afternoon until daylight faded. An intelligent, commendable lady whom I would have married if we'd belonged to the same team. A man doesn't plunge into damnation on account of his feelings, isn't that right?"

No answer. Silent folk here in Reindeer Woods.

"Sorry I talk so much, blah blah blah, but I've only just returned from two weeks isolation; I caught a dangerous stomach virus on my last trip, when I was looking for rebels in the north of the country. I had to talk to many people, many, many people, to form relationships, to be known as someone I'm not. In this case, a sentimental singing teacher who worked in a crowded school and shot Amor's arrow in every direction in the teachers' lounge—until the virus took hold of me, yet another disaster, and no need to infect the whole regiment because of this thing, so I was sent straight to isolation, where I read heaps of kids' books. Why kids' books? Well, you see, the regiment came across a valuable children's books library, and I don't know what will become of it, but at least a great part of it is here, inside my head, which forgets nothing. Then the time before last I got a hernia in a parachute jump . . . so my recitation continues. I am terribly accident-prone but fortunately, fortunately, I smile and am happy, I'm incredibly quick to recover. Like a circus freak. There are these ape genes inside me which see to it that my body repairs itself amazingly quickly, blah blah blah, I sure can talk, blah blah blah. I l o v e country air."

Billie brought up the rear. It was a great honor for her to

carry the army boot in one hand and the guitar case in the other. She would talk about this: Well, hmm, listen carefully to me, good people, though it doesn't matter to me if you don't listen, but it was in summer . . . in summer . . . last summer . . . about that summer, dear audience, it was the summer . . . more precisely, last July 3ʳᵈ, when I held a guitar case in one hand and a real soldier's boot from a real parachutist in the other. That's how it was . . . rain drops as light as leaves ran down from the heavens and wet the walkers' faces and their hair.

*xvii.* "Did this one commit suicide?" the parachutist asked when he saw the chicken hanging from the post, and he burst out laughing. As with comforters and pillows, it's good to air out your esophagus, seldom more so than when you've twisted your foot. Rafael didn't break a smile.

"You could say," he answered immediately, "the chicken's death is meant to be a preventative measure. The chickens crapped all over the lower story. Now they'll never dare shit there again." Then he carried the provisions from the black case into the house in two black plastic bags. Peter sat in the rocking chair, sighed, and rested his twisted foot on the corduroy yellow footstool. The foot looked a bit like the arm on the record player. Underneath his leather jacket he wore a white t-shirt, and under the white shirt was a noticeable little paunch. Billie set the guitar case down carefully, put the lone army boot ceremoniously in the shoe rack behind the front door, and sat, on her best behavior, on the lower steps of the stairs, awaiting further developments with her hands under her chin, electing to be invisible.

Rafael hung his army jacket up on the orange hook above the shoe rack and pulled the blue turtleneck sweater down past his waistband; he still hadn't taken off his shoes. He served coffee and cinnamon buns on a brown tray, then fetched some chocolate from one of the bags in the shipment, bringing it to the girl, and some whisky, which he poured into two water glasses; he sat down on the sofa in the living room, sighed in the same way Peter had sighed, rubbed his belly through the blue turtleneck sweater, and said, "This is firewater." Rafael drained the contents of the whisky glass. Peter poured the guts of the glass into his coffee cup and thirstily drank the whisky and coffee in one big gulp:

"The drink of fire, fire's crackle and burst," he said.

Billie looked down at her pink canvas shoes. She was partly occupied in thinking about all the chocolate she'd eaten in her life. How much space would that cover? At least over the hall floor, the living room, and the kitchen. Perhaps every single bar of chocolate which had gone inside her could cover all the grass from the front of the house up to the garden gate. Would it be possible to spread all the chocolate she had eaten over a whole football field? Had she eaten enough chocolate? Should she not eat this chocolate bar? She discovered that one of the men sitting inside the room was looking at her intently, wanting her to move away, to take herself out of listening range—the grown-ups' private time had arrived—but Billie didn't budge. Instead, she took the paper off the chocolate.

Rafael: Well, do you think you outrank me, or do I outrank you?

Peter: I was going to ask the same thing.

Rafael: I'd assumed we're the same rank.

Peter: I'd assumed so too. I don't mean to be rude, you could classify my next question as rude, which it isn't in any manner meant to be, it's related directly to my work as the army's surveyor. I trust you, sir, absolutely. But it does arouse my curiosity, sir, I'd like to know, where are members A and B of infantry division B-3 deployed?

Rafael: That's the heart of the matter. I simply don't know.

Peter: Our deployment device indicates that all the members of the team were stationed in the same place.

Rafael: Yes, that's the heart of the matter. They left me behind, alone. With the girl. They left the backpack with everything in it and had vanished when I awoke the morning after our first night here.

Peter: Well, sir, do you have any idea where they could have fled to or whether they had anything else planned?

Rafael: No idea. It was as though the earth had swallowed them. Will you please stop addressing me so formally?

Peter: Whatever you say, amigo. There've been very few deserters in this war. Interesting to hear about two. After all this time. Remarkable.

Rafael: This valley invites one to escape. There's such a great sense of freedom here. You feel it right away. The valley has an incredible effect on you.

Peter: I'm beginning to see that. This girl, this Billie, was she alone here when you all came to the farm?

Rafael: Yes.

Wholly indifferent, the cat padded from the room, to go outside to play with the fireflies in the dark.

Peter: Have you worked out how long she'd been here alone?

Rafael: Not long. I guess. At the least, she's suffered a very great shock, that's for sure.

Peter: Mhm.

Rafael: But she's holding up well.

Peter: It would have been best if you had let us know.

Rafael: How nice to know in hindsight. I felt utterly rejected when my comrades abandoned me in the house with an eleven-year-old girl, some chickens, a cow, and a cat. What option did I have? Call command and say: Hi, C, B-3, OP-17, I am stuck on a farmstead, babysitting an eleven-year-old girl in the absence of her nannies, any guardian. I'm a substitute at a home for children, but I'll come back when I'm done looking after her.

The men laughed.

Peter: Yes, I understand. A native babysitter. That is somewhat absurd. Not easy to discuss such a situation on the phone. Interesting. Very interesting. A veritable theater of the absurd. A summerhouse of loneliness. They wouldn't have believed you. They'd have considered you mentally ill and classified you at once as a deserter. I understand your reasoning completely. They tried to call your cellular phone but there was no connection—the region's telecommunications mast has been destroyed. You would never have been able to call them. It checks out. You have conducted yourself excellently, Rafael. Occupied quite a good farm and a wonderful valley, according to your description. Let the others try to do better. Now, do you feel like fetching your handicapped comrade the guitar?

Rafael: Look here, comrade, you're talking down to me. It seems that I'm under interrogation. As though I'm your prisoner.

Peter: Calm down, amigo. You're in shock. Your comrades abandoned you.

The recent arrival strummed on the guitar and called out to Billie, who stood up lazily, unsure whether she should take off her shoes. She stood there in that position and tried to make up her mind: take off her shoes, don't take off her shoes, take off her shoes, don't take off her shoes, the men wearing army boots, one with one bare foot and one not bare, take off her shoes, don't take off her shoes, she took off her shoes and padded into the room on the balls of her feet.

"Billie, do you have any musical requests?" asked the guitar player.

"I had a musical request just the day before yesterday."

"What was your musical request the day before yesterday?"

Billie put her hands on her hips and sang:

>My girl who cries
>Always at night
>Thinks I was joking
>When I made her
>But my little bundle
>My little bundle
>I was truly earnest
>When you were born

>My girl who cries
>Always at night
>Thinks God was joking
>When he made her
>But my little bundle
>My little bundle
>God intended only good
>When you were born

"How interesting, a truly remarkable, highly original work," said Peter, and laughed loudly. Without a pause, he picked up the tune as he'd promised, flowed through the melody and tra-la-la'ed along with it. Then he asked Billie to sing along. Billie cleared her throat. She curtsied. She put her hands behind her back, swung her shoulders, and sang both stanzas to the accompaniment of the parachutist. The comrades both applauded once the song was done and made a hullabaloo. She curtsied again. Then she was sent to bed with another bar of chocolate from the black bags, the black case, that black Easter egg a great bird had laid mid-flight. She took her pink canvas shoes up with her and set them on the orange chest of drawers, which lost its color once the light was turned off.

## *xviii.*

Soffia: Billie, do you think I was joking when I made you?

Abraham: Billie, do you think I was joking when I made you?

Marius: Billie, do you think God was joking when he made you?

The three: Creation reached its end, reached its end with your birth. Reached its end with her birth, Billie, Billie, Billie.

Marius: Billie, do you think it's strange, being sent into this world?

Billie: Yes, a little.

Marius: Do you feel like you've been cast into a story some-one else made up?

Billie: Yes, a little.

Marius: That's because the story needs you to come and help it. The story is missing a girl like you.

Soffia and Abraham: The story is missing a girl like you. The story is missing a girl like you. Because we weren't joking when we made you, though we'd made our way through two, three bottles of red wine, or four, or five.

Soffia: Your father was unshaven and I was uncombed, smelling of sweat.

The three: Because we were not joking, we were not confused or playing, mucking around, not on a bender when we made you. Weren't joking, weren't joking, weren't joking about when we made you. Reached its end, reached its end, reached its end with your birth.

Billie applauded them: Thank you very much, people.

Soffia, Abraham, and Marius curtsied.

The guitar player appeared and curtsied.

Rafael appeared and sang solo: I was not joking when I spared you from my gunshots. I was not joking when I allowed you to adorn creation.

The other guy: Tra la la la la tra la la la la tra la la la la.

All of them: We were not joking when we made you. We were not joking when we made you. We were not joking, truly en- en- ended with your birth, my Billie. *Bing.*

*xix.* The soldiers sang late into the night, accompanied by the guitar: quatrains, ballads, military songs, rock, and blues, and then they put albums on the record player. The girl slept and woke at intervals until everything grew quiet and she knew she was wide-awake in the silence. No one was lying on the mattress, but in the bathroom water was running into the bathtub. Then the tap was turned off.

P: Men give off a very strong smell of sweaty feet. The smell of sweaty feet on women is milder.

R: The army ought to develop a cream for sweaty feet, to get rid of the thick stench in military buildings. A spray in a convenient package that you could store in a backpack. The army has powerful scientific resources. It could be a good challenge for a young and ambitious chemist.

P: A man needs a wife to balance his bodily smells. Otherwise he gives off a stench. Animals perceive that stench and so does womankind. To hell with that crap. A man's smell gives away his spiritual condition. Each man's smell is his cunning enemy, it gossips about him.

R: Do you see how big my toes are, absolute honkers. The biggest toes in the army, for sure. They remind me of potatoes.

P: They say a man should sleep in the enemy's bed while dirty, in order to infect it with his own bodily stench and the whiff of his toes. To win the war, spread your filthy toe-stench in the enemy's bed. But that won't defeat anyone nowadays; people are always replacing things, getting newer and fresher mattresses and furniture. Far too much tidiness; it wipes away manly bravery. Tidiness kills a man's ambition. You know. Waft the stench of your toes in the enemy's direction.

R: It has something to do with gravity, the way a bad smell drops down to a man's toes and stays there. Which is a good thing, of course, imagine if a man's head smelled that terrible. The smell of unwashed hair is good. But why is the smell of men's toes different from women? Does gravity pull harder on men?

P: Old crones, now, they sweat like I don't know what. They give off a tremendous sweat stench. I love manly sweat. It's honest and bold.

R: So gravity doesn't pull equally hard on women.

P: The moon pulls on women.

R: Because of this, women have more of a sweat smell than a toe stench. It follows that the moon pulls on them and the earth on us. Because of this we want to die. The grave pulls on us. Because of this, women have more lust for life.

P: I can put up with a man's sweat-smell much better. It's invigorating, like champagne.

R: You already said that.

P: Can't a man repeat himself?

R: As far as I'm concerned, you can do what you want, providing it doesn't harm me.

P: I repeat myself because no one listens to me.

R: I listen to you.

P: You're a remarkable and interesting fellow, Rafael.

R: Take a sip. It feels good to drink whisky in a foot bath. Don't you think? Don't you think?


# *xix. (cont.)*

P: Yum. Good.

R: I can't break the habit of having a foot bath before I go to bed. It's also wonderful to have a foot bath when you're drunk because you get such a rush to your head. The hotter the water in the foot bath, the more the rush.

P: Let's add hot water. Let's add hot water.

R: It's also good for your injured foot.

The water began to run in the bathtub. The tap was turned off.

R: Have a sip while the water is boiling, boiling hot. A big slurp, then rinse your mouth with the drink.

P: Yum. My grandmother would be happy if she saw me now—she was a neat-and-tidy person. Everyone in my family is a slob. She was very lonely but I didn't pay attention to that until after she died. Lonely in the company of slobs. If I'd paid attention to that earlier I would have become a neat-and-tidy person while she was alive.

R: That's one thing the army teaches a man: to spruce himself up, to go around clean and washed and in good health.

P: Yes.

R: To iron his clothes.

P: To take a foot bath.

R: To take a foot bath.

P: To put bath salts in the foot bath.

R: No, I learned that somewhere else, I didn't learn that in the army.

P: Even when I was just a little nipper I was worried my grandmother would die. And then she died. It was a frightening loss. If I had one wish, I'd wish she could see me now in a foot bath with a good comrade. My company is of the better sort. I didn't have friends when I was little, by the devil I was so friendless. We never listened to her. No one listened to old grandma. She was like a radio broadcasting in a trash dump.

R: And so you feel no one listens to you.

P: Yes. Guilt returns to haunt the guilty, isn't that how the saying goes?

R: But I listen to you even when what you're saying is ridiculous.

P: You listen to me because you're insecure.

R: I am not untrustworthy.

P: Sure you are. I'm not really into self-confident people.

Self-confident people are hypocrites. You're my kind of guy, Raffi.

R: When I think about it, I enjoy the stench of my toes. I could consider eating wet, toe-stinking socks, socks that have just been taken out of their shoes, socks that have recently been used for a run in a heatwave. I reckon I could eat them with green or red beans. Red. Burned beans.

P: There must be something to that; otherwise the stench of toes wouldn't exist.

R: Toe-scented socks are very attractive. I will bury a wretched toe-smelling sock in the earth and write on the headstone: Here lies a glorious, toe-smelling sock, may it be remembered for eternity.

P: I know what you mean, incredible. I'd lie with toe-scented socks in the palm of my hand, close to my cheek, sleeping like a ruffian.

R: Like with a baby's bottle. Like with a baby's bottle.

P: Yes. Suck it like a popsicle. My beloved toe-fragrant socks, never leave me. I love you, I love you, I love you.

R: You have to get out while the water is still burning bubbling boiling hot. I'll help you so you don't slip on the bottom, comrade. Like this, fella.

## xix. (cont.)

P: Man, it feels good to take a piss after a foot bath.

R: Yes. It also feels good to brush one's teeth.

P: We are far too clean to go to sleep, Raffi. I'm ashamed of myself for my family's sake. How might we get ourselves filthy? Let's get ourselves filthy, Raffi. I want to be dirty. This is a theater of the absurd, a summerhouse of loneliness. I long to fall sick with love, and to crawl alternately in the dust of my love and the dust of my fatherland. This is prissy. I don't want to be here. I don't want to be clean. I'm as good as dead. Let them horsewhip me. I am a total fool. I'm eaten up by stupidity. The devil's babble. The summerhouse of loneliness. I long to have my testicles cut off and placed in the National Museum. Cyclone, blow Raffi and me away from the brown trash dump and hang our testicles in the National Museum. The testicles of a parachutist. My good God. The brain of a parachutist. The toes of a parachutist. Blub blub blub. A whole glass cage in the National Museum, with my body parts divided into their single pieces. For my fatherland. The heart of a parachutist. The legs of a parachutist. But Raffi, my member wouldn't be there, because it will be eaten by wolves. Our enemies might retrieve it. I promise you that—

R: Have some whisky, Petey guy. Feel how good it is to have whisky in your mouth when your teeth are freshly brushed.

P: Delightful.

R: Don't spit at me, man.

P: No, my apologies, I'm talking nonsense. Now I feel like a chicken or a missionary. It's not possible to win the war with newly-washed toes. I'll pour whisky over my toes.

R: Good idea. Me too. Good idea.

P: I'm still the same old slob, even though grandmother is dead and the army has taught me class-conscious cleanliness. Forgive me, grandmother, since I cannot be like you, amen. A man is only clean in training. Then, when he comes out onto the battlefield, it's best to relax one's standards, which are no use to anyone at that moment. I'm going to write a book called

69

*How To Win War With Tidiness*, i.e. that's how one loses its. *Uncleanliness on the Battlefield*, that's what's I'll call it. The basic requirement for victory is filth. Physical filth. Dirty toes. Stench of sweat, lice.

R: Don't be a fool. Come on, my friend.

P: Pinworms and goldworms.

R: Enjoy relaxing in the country air, Petey.

The door to the bathroom opened and rays of light flickered on the girl's eyelids.

P: I think everyone is a slob, except the dead. Even though one doesn't shower after death—who regrets that? Just imagine, Raffi: skeletons in a shower. Spirits in a bath. I'd like to soap a skeleton, some skeleton, from the crown to the soles. That's definitely fucking fun. Hey skeleton, may I soap your palms now? Wow. To lie in a bath with a skeleton. Some time, we should skin our enemies and put them with . . . Am I to believe you sleep on the mattress in the child's room? Raffi, comrade.

R: Where else would I sleep? She could run away. Remember that she is partly a prisoner of war.

P: That's remarkable. Interesting. What should the army do with such a girl?

R: Yes, what do you reckon?

P: I have to explore this territory, find infantry division B-3— I've got that finished, at least part of the team—write a report about operation OP-17; I have no idea what one should do with prisoners of war who are children. The problem with war is that one doesn't know what to do with the children.

R: This girl is the radiance in this land. The light of her generation. We can't kill her.

Rafael snuck barefoot into the bedroom, the cuffs on his army pants turned up, his toes freshly washed. There were hints of the scent of the olive soap and striped blue toothpaste, and the hours-old stink of tobacco and whisky.

P: I agree. Rather we lose the war than kill Billie.

R: Wow, the girl has made my bedclothes so beautifully. I can't show you, unfortunately, because I haven't the heart to turn on the light. A kid melts a man's heart. Like the animals. The kids and the animals are complete puzzles.

P: She is a national treasure, like the pyramids of Egypt.

# *xix. (cont.)* Rafael clambered across the mattress with the army-issue comforter in his arms and closed the door. From the sound of it, the men were undressing in the big bedroom where Marius had gone to bed for five hundred days, always after completing his impressive walking tour of the house's living spaces in his night shirt. He would begin on the lower story, closing curtains where there were curtains, paying attention to the electric outlets—he thought it safest to jerk all plugs from their outlets overnight, though not the fridge or the radio alarm clocks by his bed and by Jenny and Inga's bed. He checked whether people had forgotten to turn off the stovetop or the oven, the iron, the iron, he disconnected it if perhaps it had been forgotten. He checked on the electric heater and boiler when it was cold outside. He turned the water faucets fully off and sometimes he turned off the water during the night, you could never be too careful. He checked whether the windows were closed, since they might otherwise

blow open with an untimely gust of wind. The fridge closed, the fridge closed. The door closed; there was no need to lock it, but because he had lived in the city he tended to lock the door out of habit; he had to remind himself how things were in the country as he stood there struggling to leave the door unlocked. He put out all the lights downstairs except for the blue-and-white battery-lamp in the kitchen window, and then he snuck upstairs barefoot. Peeked in on the kids, checked whether some of them had gone to sleep with the light on, arranged the quilts, checked whether a comforter or a pillow was touching the hot light-bulb or radiator. He turned the taps in the bathroom off more firmly, both the little kid sink and the larger grown-up sink, checking whether the taps had unintentionally been left dripping, which might lead to water loss. He turned out the ceiling lights in the corridor but then lit the green wall lamp.

Marius loved to be the last one up, late in the evening, after he'd checked on everything and everyone. This tour of the house was the high point of his day. It was his life's mission to leave the house, the electricity, the heat, the water, the kids sleeping like stones, and the women too, he himself, the pipes, and the windows, all of them in the safe hands of the night. The last barefoot steps were everything to him, filling him with even more excitement and anticipation than getting up in the morning. He dried his soles on the mat on the bedroom floor before he slipped under the comforter. He closed his eyes and thought about what he'd been occupied with during the previous sixteen or seventeen hours; he mentally prepared the following day's tasks, sketched them vaguely, rough drawings in his head.

A few times Billie accompanied Marius on his evening tour because she tended to wake up when she wasn't supposed to, at least according to the rulebook. Like now. Wasn't it best if a kid like her tried to wake up only once in the solar cycle, not more often? The radio on the radio alarm clock was turned on in the big bedroom and set at low volume. It was a somewhat familiar rock song. Billie disappeared into a dream about a spring-man who was wearing the same clothes as the parachutist. A black leather jacket with fur on the neck collar.

> Hi Billie I am the spring-man, there are 365 days
> in the year, want some gum?
> Hi Billie I am the spring-man, there are 365 days
> in the year, want some gum?
> Hi Billie I am the spring-man, there are 365 days
> in the year, want some gum?

**XX.** The secret spy wearing rabbit slippers ought to wake early to study the evidence of the night. The front door stood wide open. Lots of cigarettes had been smoked in the living room, since the soldiers had plenty of them, but they'd also tidied, washed up, cleaned all the ashtrays, set the guitar next to the telephone in hall, the Barbie dolls in the rocking chair—what were her Barbie dolls doing in the rocking chair? There were empty beer cans in a black plastic bag out by the doorstep. Billie weighed the bag. The dead hen lay in a bath of water with a sliced lemon in a big pot on the kitchen stove; the girl could see that because she got up onto a chair. On the fridge hung a picture of a finely dressed and neat middle-aged man. How much could grown-ups get done in one night while the kids slept?

Behind the kitchen table she found the other black bag; it was filled with countless cans of beer, whisky bottles, chocolate bars, cigarette cartons—never had she seen so many privately-owned cigarette cartons—gas masks, dried meat, soup packets, powdered milk, medicine, bandages, bank notes in a thick plastic bag with a zipper, bath soap, shaving cream, razors, toilet paper, tea and coffee. Against the wishes of the labor legislation, which frees children from bondage (how peculiar that you can't force a child to work but children are forced to study—perhaps so they can read voting ballots), Billie stood back up on the chair at the kitchen stove, heating water and brewing coffee. She wanted to become part of the group, too, especially when the others had done so well. To show solidarity with their efforts to keep the home tidy and elegant.

As the aroma of her coffee, her virgin coffee, traveled up the stairs, Rafael came down. They met midway. The man: Good day, coffee. Coffee aroma: Good day, sir, or farmer, are you a soldier or are you a farmer today? Sir: No interrogation so early in the day, dear coffee.

Wearing the farmer's nightshirt, Rafael brushed sleep, little clods, frostroses, crease tears, crow's pus, fluff, dream-waste, dream-slush, space-dust from his eyes; he was barefoot, and there was toothpaste on one corner of his mouth.

"You've come at exactly the right moment for coffee," said Billie.

"Thank you, my big little dame," said Rafael, and he sat. She handed him the steaming hot coffee. "Our friend has now departed. His mission in Reindeer Woods is over. But he left the guitar behind and taught me two chords, which should be enough for any tunes. We found an old bicycle outside the shed. In fact, it wasn't old. Do you know who owned it?"

"No," she answered, to the best of her knowledge.

"He decided to cycle away from the valley, get a complete picture of the region and then cycle west to Forever Valley. From there it's a day's journey, maybe two, to the next military airport."

"Will we see him again?" asked Billie, who had looked forward to giving the man coffee. But things just had to be as they were; that's how they'd happened. Still, it would have been fun to give him coffee. Perhaps he would have smiled that wonderful, curious smile.

"Not in the short run, at least."

"It's nice that he let us have the guitar," she said, looking at it.

"Yes," replied Rafael, and he, too, looked at the guitar, which reddened under all the attention, so that the case grew warm, and when a draft of wind came through the open living room window and front door it sounded like the last chords of a rock song. Billie watched the wind's journey from the room, through the hall, and outside. How strange it was that the parachutist should decide to cycle away wearing one shoe—the army boot still stood in the shoe-rack where she'd placed it the evening before. Perhaps Peter had blue flip flops, like Rafael, a gift from the army. Or cycled away from the valley in one army boot and one flip flop. Better to cycle than to walk when you've turned your ankle, especially if you laugh when you see a chicken on a pole.

"Do you think it will rain?" asked Billie, a sentence she'd first heard in a movie, "I think its grand to walk in the rain."

"Me too," answered Rafael, "should we go for a walk even if it isn't raining?"

"I don't know," she replied, not wanting to make a promise she couldn't keep, like her dad, who often got mixed up thanks to the puppeteers, those beings on another planet. What's more, she'd hadn't said anything about enjoying walking in weather other than rain. She was her own guardian now, and it was too soon for a girl of her age to go for a stroll with a fully-grown man. "Mightn't there be land mines around?" she asked, with heavy eyes. "The airplane could have strewn invisible land mines over Reindeer Woods without us knowing about it."

"No, that's impossible," replied Rafael, smiling.

"Listen, fella, perhaps I'll tell you a little more about my father the puppet?"

## xx. (cont.)

"First tell me about Marius."

"When Marius graduated from the state ballet school, the National Ballet invited him to be their principal dancer. Marius hoped that Maria would become a principal dancer too, but the company didn't want Maria and Maria didn't want to be in the company. She wanted to write ballets herself and dance in them. Maria went and met with the ballet director and said: I am here to give notice that I won't be in your company. I decline to be a part of it, thanks. We never offered you anything, the ballet director said. She said, All the same, I respectfully decline. The National Ballet does not suit my direction. We never offered you anything, repeated the ballet director, but she shook her head like the man was an idiot, curtsied like the dancer she was, and strode off, her back straight as an arrow.

"She went to dance at a nightclub, so she had enough to live on, and she wrote her ballets in an ice-cold rehearsal room by day. But it wasn't because of Maria that Marius left the company. He got tired of the staring, and he said so to Maria one night when they were going to sleep in her bedroom—she slept in his nightclothes and he in her nightclothes because they were romantic, and a bit sentimental, too. He wore her cream and she wore his cream. She became anxious if she didn't have his smell close by, but if he felt anxious he took pain medicine. But on with the story: One night, he said to Maria that it was like being a stripper, dancing on the stage of the National Ballet, and he just didn't feel like being a stripper for the State and for smart and powerful people and for clever people in the city. That's such ingratitude from one of the most talented ballet dancers of our age, said Maria, and got mad, and the quarrel woke up her roommate, who started crying. She couldn't listen to this quarrel because she thought an all-out war had begun." Billie instinctively lowered her voice:

"I ought to say that Maria actually was a stripper, more or less, like a go-go dancer at a nightclub. All the girls in a row lifting up their skirts. She didn't allow Marius to come see her dance in the nightclub. He was only allowed to see her dance in her studio, where she composed her ballets. Marius winced: I dance classical ballet, which has one purpose, to act like a living waxwork for a dead culture, like talking Latin into an answering machine all day long. Am I really meant to devote my body to training for a world order I dislike? I don't like the situation, no sir. I am a living ruin, a monument of a dead past and an oppressive force in the present, and as long as my body is young and strong, I shan't be a living ruin again. The spectators who come to see us in the National Ballet are too elegant to sit in a nightclub, too frightened of infections and scared of thieves, so instead they go to an art museum to gape at statues and to the theater to watch ballet.

"That's what Marius had to say. Maria said that Marius had gone mad. Marius left the ballet and moved out of the room he rented, bought a little house in the outskirts; then, finally, he was content. He asked Maria to move in. There was enough space for her to write ballets. He would take her to work at the club and wait for her and drive her back home. Watch her produce the ballets and be her dramaturge. He'd prepare hot food for her at lunchtime. Marius went to the store to shop every day until he moved to Reindeer Woods. Food and painkillers. And this spring he tipped all the pain medicine into the ground to see if it would grow into flowers or a painkiller tree. Nothing has come up yet."

"That was optimistic. How did Marius earn money?"

"From his father. He'd never had money of his own, but all of a sudden he sent Marius money right before he died, to appease his conscience. Isn't that what it's called when people act like that, appeasing a conscience?"

"Indeed."

"But Maria didn't want to live with Marius. She wanted instead to live in the little rented bedroom and cycle to her job at the club. Do you know why she said no?"

"No."

"Because each person has to go and thread her own crow-path. She often said so to Marius, who kept repeating this sentence time and again. Each person ought to thread her own crow-path. He often said it unprovoked, when he was fixing porridge, putting the laundry in the washing machine. I said that if he continued to repeat this sentence, one day it would catch fire inside him, and his body would burn in a clear, inextinguishable fire. Then he tried to stop but he couldn't, and said: If I stop saying it, then I'll have to begin taking painkillers again. The sentence saves me from pain medication. Well then, I said, you should just drink water every time you say it. That's a defense against fire inside you. Or else it will dry you up."

"And?"

"Marius loved his little house and everything around it. The people in the nearby houses, the people in the drugstores and other stores, and the King of Rock who lived in the house opposite. When the war began he got his mother and his aunt to move in together, and he sold the little house. The King of Rock also gave him money. They had become friends ever since the lampposts; they both wanted to get new lampposts on their street, ones with softer light bulbs—the stark light had been keeping everyone awake—and one night the King of Rock had planned to shoot out the bulbs with a gun, but Marius calmed the King down. They would play billiards together when the King's friend was painting the laundry room floor. The King of Rock couldn't go a single day without billiards. Before Marius moved here, he told Maria that there would always be a space for her with the children in Reindeer Woods, forever. Then he didn't hear from her for 366 days, and still there's no news of her. Perhaps she is stuck on her crow-path."

"Did Marius stop dancing entirely, then?"

"Yes. What's more, he got a little fat. You get fat if you suddenly stop dancing, but he didn't stop walking with splayed feet."

"Go on."

## XX. (cont.)

"One morning when Marius was tending the rose-bed in front of the French windows, I was sitting in the grass. Marius, I have fallen in love with you, I said. I wanted to know what it's like to say that to someone who wasn't totally familiar, someone who wasn't family. The way it's said in movies. The actors have to be in love even with strangers. Marius stopped pulling weeds and looked at me. Billie, he said as he stared right at me, I've stopped pursuing my love life. Not just because Maria hasn't come. I am not so pushy that if I don't get the person I love then I don't want anyone. No no no. I want to bind everyone to me I can think to bind to me, with one condition: that the ties might vanish as quickly as night becomes day. The more time you spend with someone the stronger the bonds become, ever more tangled and difficult to unravel when you want to get loose. Like with Maria. I waited all that time, and after that more time passed, and the thread still connects us, completely for my part. I doubt it will ever vanish. That means that if I enter into a love affair with other people, all kinds of threads and wires will extend from my heart, and I would have to attend to all those wires, even though it seems that I'm free. It would end with a whole forest of wires shooting out from my heart. When I finally understood this, I was connected only to Maria, Mom, and Jenny. The damage had been done, and I would never be able to disconnect from them. I will never be free from these three women, and I will never add anyone else to the crowd. Never. The children leave anyway, and that's good. They grow up and leave. That's good.

"It was a long-winded speech, and I very much pitied Marius, who just kept on talking wretchedly:

"My mom is independent and free because she conceived me

80

on a ski trip with a boy she didn't know. It was lucky that Dad wanted nothing to do with us, so she didn't have to negotiate and fight with her lover, former or current. My mom is my model. Yes, Marius, I said, that doesn't change the fact that I have fallen in love with you. Marius stroked my cheek. I respect your love and will guard it well, he said. A little sentimental. I: I am only eleven years old and it is illegal for us to be together, but I cannot stop being in love with you. No need to stop, he said, and he went back to pulling weeds. I went and decided to write him a love letter from his only lover, Maria, the pretty ballerina. Do you want to know what I wrote in the love letter?"

"Yes, why not," said Rafael.

"My love, each dance-step I take on the dance floor, I take for you. Yours for eternity, Maria. I cut out the letters, arranged them, pasted them on paper, and put the paper in an envelope. I addressed the envelope: Marius, love angel, and placed it on the desk in the office. Then came the reply. It was lying in my boot in a white envelope addressed in red letters: Maria. Since it was in my boot I was allowed to read it:

"My love, I know that you don't dance for anyone but me and never will. Each time you sleep with other men you sleep with me. The ballet you compose is for my eyes only and in my memory. Year after year you meet with my deputies, and on the first day with each guy you pretend you have never lived such a day. That's the way the magical power of fantasy works. Our love has no time limits, no borders between life and death. Yours for eternity, Marius."

"Wow," said the soldier, squinting his eyes because he desperately wanted some headache medicine, which he was looking for in the black bag full of supplies from the army.

"I wrote a letter in reply:

"My love, Marius. You will not get me because I am like the wind. My dancing is also like that. The wind is my model. You love me the way a man loves the wind. With thanks for all. Your Maria."

"Did you receive a reply?" Rafael popped the headache pills into his mouth.

"Dear Maria, my dearest saint. You are the wind and I am the rain which falls to earth and hides itself from the sunshine. At times I move with the wind in an embrace and that's bliss. The rain travels the world and cleans the streets, waters the plants and washes people's faces. The wind shifts itself and shifts everything it touches, skirts and overcoats and caps, which blow away into the blue. I love you my tender angel-body. The night we awakened to the smell of cakes from the bakery was and is the peak of my journey as a lover. It will not be repeated. Love is for teenagers, Maria, I am precocious. I will spend my life getting old and enjoy it without having my lover's eyes see my body decay. I don't feel like waiting. I want to age immediately and let those who are younger enjoy this wonderful moment of love which the world is full of, which explodes out of it like some crazy bubble machine. I hope everyone will discover that moment; I hope everyone enjoys its wonderful journey and many delights. You also, Maria, and your imagination. I will never forget our mornings, yours always, your friend and lover, Marius the former ballet dancer, now a vegetable gardener and friend to children."

"Oof," said Rafael, and he stared at Billie.

"Maria said that Marius ought to see a doctor about the depression, but he didn't understand what she meant. I am not depressed, he said, I know what I want, I want to be in peace away from human life."

"He said that?"

"Yes: That's not my cup of tea, it's your cup of tea, human life in the city is your cup of tea, the ballet and things, not my cup of tea."

"Remarkable: an amazing and curious perspective. Wasn't he like the spectators at the National Ballet then, the elegant and powerful people who avoid life, perhaps out of a deep-rooted fear of infection?"

"Well," answered Billie solemnly. "One could say that."

"Awkward."

"Marius loved to make sure we kids were secure. To make sure that we didn't burn up in the house and stuff. Have you noticed how many fire extinguishers there are on the farm?"

"And?"

"He put the fire extinguishers up with an electric drill his friend the King of Rock gave him as a parting gift."

"That's very thoughtful of him," said Rafael, standing up, and he poured the contents of the wine-red thermos flask into the cup and belched quietly, as you do when you're a little bloated. Then he finished the rest of the virgin coffee, Billie's coffee, in one gulp.

## xxi.

"Tell me about your dad the puppet."

"One night mom was working, as she often did, in the emergency room, and she had been awake for more than twenty-four hours when she was ordered to take a look at the patient in room twelve. There sat my expectant father-to-be, just as sleepy as she was, hunched and with his arm in his lap. He held out his arm to mom: Would you sew it on? How would I sew . . . Mom examined his arm, which was totally bloodless, strangely enough. With an ordinary needle and thread, said Dad. It could be yarn or fishing line. As long as it hangs down beside me, my companions will see about the rest.

"What rest? What companions? asked Mom, but Dad told her not to ask him such tangled questions—he was exhausted after the night he'd had. They were both dead sleepy and that might have affected their judgment. Perhaps they wouldn't have gotten to know each other if they'd met when they were well-rested. What do you do for a living? asked Mom once she'd begun sewing the arm to the shoulder; she longed to hear some crazy crime stories. Because he wore gold rings on his fingers and was dressed in a jacket and a fine white shirt with a silk tie and gold shirt buttons, she thought Dad was a criminal. He said he was a jurist. How was your arm torn off like this? I'm asking you, sir, because I need to write a report about you.

"They quarreled over me, my companions who very spite-fully control me—Mom immediately understood this to mean that Dad's aforementioned companions were criminals. One wanted me to go to the nightclub, another wanted me to go home. They quarreled and tugged at me until my arm came off. The one who wanted to go to the club controlled the arm you're fastening back on. The other wanted to go home to write down my thoughts about jurisprudence and wisdom. Indeed, I came to a remarkable realization tonight which could change all of my work, turn it clean on its head.

"What realization? asked my mom, curiously.

"That crimes don't exist, said Dad.

"Bingo, thought Mom, I knew he was involved with crime. How's that? she asked, waiting to hear how he would justify himself and his criminal companions.

"Crimes are contracts, social agreements, said Dad. Who owns planet earth? No one. Why, then, is it possible to buy bits of it, three hectares or so, and own them and hang those who come and steal splinters from it?

"Do you mean, sir, that robbers are innocent? asked mom.

"Dad nodded his head, but he was too tired to talk further—when puppets get tired, then puppets get tired.

"It's a crime to murder someone, said Mom.

"For you, every life is sacred, you're a doctor, said Dad—but I will develop my theory better when I sit down to write. It would be best if I didn't have the arm reattached, since it always wants to go to the nightclub—and yet without it I wouldn't be able to balance and I would have to be in a wheelchair, but since my apartment is upstairs on the fifth story, I couldn't get there in a wheelchair, and that's where my manuscript of jurisprudence awaits me. Then he dozed off and Mom continued sewing, convinced that this man was both a sincere and a wily criminal."

The sun pierced through the kitchen window, and Rafael pinched Billie on the nose. It embarrassed her—a narrator shouldn't be disturbed—but then again a narrator wasn't allowed to react sensitively. "Thanks for the coffee and the stories," he said, "the time has come to stand up and take care of the farm work."

"The time has come to clear one's throat," said Billie, and she cleared her throat.

Rafael stood up and went on his usual morning route: feeding the chickens, milking the cow, examining the vegetable garden, going into the greenhouse to nurse and water the greenhouse plants, feeding the cat, painting the gutter on the shed, picking up cow dung from the grass, fastening the windows, all those mundane chores which have to get done on a farm.

Thanks to the labor legislation—the article regarding paid and unpaid work by children—Billie avoided farm work like the plague, and had the legal right to do so. In the upstairs bedroom, she put on her denim clothes. They were muddy, but that was just fine. At the front door she put on her pink canvas shoes and her yellow cap, which she found in the hat basket next to the shoe-rack where the lone soldier's boot had been left behind—she put the rabbit-head slippers beside it. They usually waited here for her all day on outdoor days. On indoor days, they warmed her feet and toes.

She dawdled about the plot up away from the house. She had her hands in her pockets. Her four fingers were polishing a green stone. It was an eternal task. When she became big, whenever that was, she'd still be polishing it. She would keep the stone in the pocket of the grown-up's overcoat she'd wear one day. It would become Billie's own personal experiment, to see how her fingertips could smooth a stone over the course of years. Further down from the garden gate, someone had cleared a parking area which could easily fit five, maybe six, cars; beyond that stood an old brick garage, beside which lay a path across to the highway. The orange car was parked in front of the shed. She peered into the car, in case she might find something there, a reward. She tried to open the trunk. It was unlocked, stuffed with camping gear, sleeping bags, a tent, a fishing rod, and a Primus stove. Then she scooted under the car and lay there on her back with her hands touching her sides. Mmmmmm. That was the best bed. An excellent cover. The aroma, mmmmm so good. Oil dripped from the engine and made a black patch on the gravel.

Billie turned over onto her stomach and watched as a royal blue automobile came down the path from the highway, which was road number thirteen and ended in the valley—it barely deserved to be called a highway. The automobile stopped directly in front of the fine carved garden gate.

> The Children in Reindeer Woods welcome you
> Allow the children to come to me
> All children are the children of God
> All the gods are gods of children

A picture of children sitting on a reindeer that had stopped for a rest, standing next to swans in green reeds.

*XXII.* Billie ambled down the path, swinging her arms back and forth and acting as though things on the farm were full of such great comings-and-goings that she was mostly unaffected by them and had little better to do than to idle about. She thought she'd learned to behave like a farm-girl quite well from movies, a mix between a street kid and a lollygagging, well-looked-after darling. Two tall men got out of the automobile and stood beside it. They were taller and thinner than Rafael, and yet nowhere near as tall and slim as Abraham; few people could match her dad's height or figure. Perhaps they were about Marius's build. They wore smart suits, pale pink shirts, and light blue ties. Rafael appeared from the back garden—he'd abandoned his soldier's civilized gait—wearing the farmer's light overalls, a white t-shirt and rubber boots. A religious symbol hung on a chain around his neck; he might have been rummaging around in Marius's nightstand.

He set a red gasoline can down and fished a red handkerchief out of his trouser pocket, which he used to dry the beads of sweat on his forehead. One of the men combed his hair. The cat padded over to Rafael. Rafael stuffed the cloth in his pocket and picked the cat up in his arms. Likewise, the girl thought to stroll nonchalantly past and climb up onto the roof of the shed. There was a good view. She kept an eye out for guns. The other man took an envelope from his jacket pocket and opened the letter inside.

"So the war hasn't reached here yet?" he asked.

Rafael nodded his head.

"You know there is a war going on?" the man asked next.

"Yes, well enough," answered Rafael, nodding his head several times.

"It's a good thing war hasn't yet reached here. On this farm live," the man read from the letter, "one, two, three . . . three adults. Four children, right, and a shepherd is registered as having his home here." He handed the letter to his colleague. "Where are these people, if we might enquire?"

"They went camping up in the mountains. Hunting and enjoying the outdoors. We are living in a summerhouse of loneliness."

"It's good that people aren't letting the war stop them from traveling, though it could, of course, cost them dearly. We are from the tax authority. They're late paying the farm tax."

"I neither worry about nor know anything about money matters on the farm."

"How many cars are registered to this home?"

The man holding the letter pointed towards where the orange car was standing.

"Two," said Rafael.

"In the letter, only one car is listed. The other needs to be documented. Which car is documented and which car isn't documented?" He looked up, peered at the letter, looked at Rafael. "Do you want to take this opportunity to document the car? Presumably, it's the car the household has taken camping."

While the two men waited for the farmer's response, one of them looked up at the shed's roof; Billie disliked him immediately. It was best not to stare at strangers, at least not in this instance.

"Can I invite you inside for coffee?" said Rafael, when he finally opened his mouth.

The two men looked at one another and nodded their heads.

"Yes, thanks, that's more than kind. It's always great to step foot inside a farmhouse. We've been sitting on black leather upholstery for five hours without a break. No stores on the route, no restaurants, no coffee-shops . . ."

Rafael released the cat, which saw its fortunes had altered and vanished at once from the yard. The guests approached the doorstep. One pointed to the army boots by the entryway: "That definitely suggests the war," he said to his companion.

"The war finds even remote places," the other answered, kicking at the black bag, which flashed empty beer cans. "Perhaps you think it strange, my young fellow, that the tax authority should take the trouble to visit an isolated farm during a war—but even though the world is out of breath, everyone must stick to his role. That's the only way we'll make it through this horseplay in one piece."

They wiped the soles of their shoes on the doormat and closed the door with evident resolve. The chickens wandered into the hen house, and the door closed after the last one. Billie backed down the roof but, as she was about to jump down to the grass, her belt-loop got caught on one of the brackets that held the gutter up—she hung in thin air, not wanting to free herself right away. She fixed the situation in her memory in case someone later asked: Billie, have you ever hung from a gutter? How was it?

*XXiii.* Four years prior to ending up in sickroom number twelve, stupid and exhausted from fatigue and blood-loss (blood-loss always afflicted the puppet), Abraham had, one spring morning, opened an empty notebook and written on the title page:

My Love Life
by Abraham Masson

N.B. A.M. is not the proprietor of the material herein
nor of the abstract phenomena or concept on this earth,
and he declines his rights to ownership and property;
it was simply the plainest and most direct title the
author could choose for his booklet.

Then he smoothed out a page and began writing:

> I have no ambition for a love life here on earth, but events have transpired such that I have met people who showed an intimate interest in my person.

By lunchtime he had filled almost eight pages, mostly dealing with his foster-mother, his foster-brothers and foster-sisters. He continued making his report:

> Part of me has loved, out of affection, a girl who worked at an unpopular pub. I was pulled towards the silence surrounding her; she was more or less mute, emotionally feeble, and last but not least unaware, which also described my own personality. The girl was friendly, and I was friendly in return. Our close acquaintance swept us up for four wonderful weeks. Part of me has loved, out of pity and compassion, a woman who I had sympathy for in my arrogance, my contempt for people and for coldness. The more I had sympathy for her, the more dependent I became on her presence, and it took me years and days to become independent. Part of me has loved, for friendship's sake, a good, kind woman and we enjoyed our love comfortably and amicably. I recommend intimate acquaintance with a friend if you prefer peaceful days. Part of me has loved through drinking with friends, out-and-out drinking buddies. I'm thankful for the opportunities I was given to enjoy physical intimacy with others, but now I set a period after them.

Abraham cut the unwritten pages out and closed the book. Four years later, Soffia opened door number twelve and looked with such great interest at the thin face of Abraham that she ran into an old coat-rack and knocked it over. She stooped, righted it, and looked up at the man. He never forgot the eyes he saw.

Crimes do not exist. I say the same thing about love. If I didn't forget you, I can thank my own particular memory, said Abraham, a few years later.

One loves out of habit, a god complex, sexual appetite, shyness, envy, and opportunism, said Soffia.

They were sitting and debating; it was one of the birthday parties they held to celebrate Vanity.

Abraham only vaguely noticed Soffia when she sewed his arm on the first time, in part because he was an ungrateful guy who had been spoiled plenty by women, and he'd stopped paying attention to each distinct event in world history. As they sewed, her fingers touched him in a gentle fashion. Because of this, he noticed her a few days later, when his body reminded him of the fingers which had tripped along his shoulder and arm as they'd worked to fasten the two together; his skin missed that touch. The next time his arm tore from his shoulder and Abraham appeared at the emergency ward, he refused to accept help from anyone but Soffia, who bumped her head against the shelf above the table where the doctors sat to fill out prescriptions, making it bleed. Abraham dried the wound with a handkerchief which he pulled out of his jacket pocket. Her body reminded her of that, of the way the man had dried her wound with the handkerchief, a few days later. Her body reminded her with the twittering we call regret. From then on, the memory in their bodies began to demand even more memories to draw from. As the saying goes, much wants more.

Abraham gathered material about jurisprudence and wisdom and went to pubs, but the pushy puppeteer, the student of taverns, controlled his movements more often than the puppeteer who wanted to sit at home and write. The third—the one who chose to lie down with Soffia all day long—was always somewhere in the middle.

One time, when Abraham's arm ripped off during a brawl between the puppeteers about what should happen, whether to go home or to the pub, Soffia refused to sew it back on; she took the torn arm and hid it. Borrowing a wheelchair was easy for a doctor, and so began a period of diligence in which Abraham sat at Soffia's home in the wheelchair and wrote his work of jurisprudence; Soffia worked her shifts, and between them she sat at home too, reading medical books and pushing Abraham around in the wheelchair. She enjoyed pushing him. He enjoyed letting her push him because he loved depending on her, a change from the time when he didn't want to depend on anyone. Amidst this peaceful medical work, writing, and reading, Billie arrived. No-one had expected that. Abraham had thought his life's mission on earth was not to have children, thought he was meant to break the mold, to exceed the frame that had been planned for him. It occurred to him that he might abandon mother and daughter before everything became too complicated and messy. Then he would leave behind a little souvenir which, amusingly enough, would grow larger, and he could fulfill his obligations as a jurist somewhere else in peace and quiet.

My love, sew my arm back on, asked Abraham.

Soffia: No, Abraham. It isn't good for you to drink beer now. Why isn't it good for me?

Your child will want you near her and I do too, Mama, Mama wants to have Papa by her. Mama is not the sort of mom who tolerates being left alone with a child.

But perhaps the child doesn't want to have a dad in a wheelchair.

Well, yes, she does. More than a dad who is not around. Also, she doesn't know what it's like to have a dad who is not in a wheelchair.

I want my child to know me as a man with two arms who can walk on his own.

Not immediately. I need you around while I'm feeding the child.

I need to drive this tension out of my body, Soffia.

Do you think I don't have tension in my body, Abraham? But Soffia didn't say: I don't want those girls in bars hanging around with you. Those girls very much enjoy playing with puppets. Instead, she said this: Each person has his golden drink, the drink which once made him the happiest fool in the world. The most glorious and freest human being. In my case, Abe, I am lucky that it's orange juice. At the first taste of orange juice, bliss rushed through my body. Afterwards, if I have more orange juice, I try to re-live this bliss; it happens occasionally and, wow, it feels good. You're unfortunate that your golden drink is beer. It would be more fortunate if your golden drink were non-alcoholic.

Why am I so unfortunate, Soffia?

I don't know that and I don't know why I don't drink my golden drink in big gulps, orange juice, time and time again, like you do with beer.

That's true, Soffia, no drink has made me as free and happy as beer. But I am just as free and happy when I breathe in the outside air early in the morning. I will never grow tired of breathing the air.

And so ended this round of the debate, but the presently passive puppeteer, the one with a thirst for taverns, began demanding that Abraham take effective measures to regain his lost arm:

I am forced to sit and stare as my companions compete to lead you, the one hypnotized by these female wiles, the other thinking about nothing but jurisprudence, while I gnaw at the backs of my hands. I am quite bored, Abraham. Help, help, help, nagged the puppeteer.

What do you want me to do? Abraham asked, very courteously.

Kill the woman, she's holding you back, boy.

I am not a boy, I am a man.

What's a man like you, a happy-go-lucky playboy, doing burrowing down with a woman and a kid?

I am not a playboy.

You've earned a twenty-eight days respite, and if the arm isn't back on its shoulder by then, you're dead meat.

Just kill me, said Abraham, since as a supporter of democracy I'm allowing the other puppeteers to manage my affairs. You have wielded power far too long.

What a load of nonsense. It's not justice that the arm I control is in storage. That's not democracy. Twenty-eight days. Mister Abraham Masson.

They had that conversation one dark night while Billie slept in the cradle dreaming abstract dreams and Soffia worked a night shift to save up for a baby carrier so they could take the newborn on a trip. First of all they wanted to visit the grandmother and grandfather, but there were more places in their plan. To look at the Temple of Love in India. To go somewhere else to debate the proposition: does love exist, does love not exist. To rent a rowboat in San Francisco, the little child in a baby carrier, and row out to the gallows island, Alcatraz. To sit there debating, arguing over the innocence of the vanished prisoners. What life is. Whether we are guinea pigs, or whether we are here of our own accord. Whether we should take things seriously. Whether we shouldn't take things seriously. Are people good. Are crimes the chain reactions of other crimes. Etc. Abraham and Soffia could begin debating by the last rays of setting sun, and when the old man sent out the first shoots of the coming day Abraham, or Soffia, would stand up to make coffee, to set a new tempo for another high-spirited debate, no, no, no, not to set a new tempo, just moisten the throat because the body obeys the mission, the mission of the debate. And why not choose different places from around the world for their topics of discussion? They needed to own a baby carrier, yet in planning their journey they hadn't discussed how to travel with a wheelchair and a lost arm.

On the first of the twenty-eight days, Abraham became energetic as never before, sitting from morning to evening over the jurisprudence manuscript, writing new pages which he gathered together with the earlier, the oldest, the somewhat older, and the somewhat new writing. He looked after little Billie. He gave her her bottle at the right time. He washed her at the right time. Everything was done like this, at the right time, so over the next days Soffia began to have second thoughts: Do I love this punctual man? she asked herself, before she remembered that love was a habit, a god complex, sexual appetite, shyness, envy, and opportunism. The last of these shamed her. Soffia totally disliked the notion, she would have given it—her own arm—not to become an opportunist. Thirteen days before the puppeteer's deadline ran out, Soffia, who knew nothing about the twenty-eight-day deadline and who wasn't in the habit of disturbing Abraham while he was writing, peeked in on him; he looked up from his writing and held tightly onto his fountain pen, fearful that someone would take the pen from him, perhaps not without reason. Soffia handed him the arm. My love, I have decided to sew it back on.

She sat down and fixed the arm to the shoulder better than she had done before—hitherto she'd been cheating on her needlework in order to make Abraham dependent on her. Now she did a better job. She sewed the arm to the shoulder using supple and unbreakable thread, the most beautiful stitches a doctor could pride herself on. I'm done, she said, cutting the twine with her teeth and knotting pretty knots at the end. Abraham stood up. Soffia pushed the wheelchair from under him and said: Best if we free ourselves from its hold immediately.

*xxiv.* Now Billie knew what it felt like to hang from the gutter by her belt loop. She wouldn't get in trouble if people asked her questions. She could answer: The summer I was eleven years old, my twelfth year, I caught the belt loop of my blue jeans on the gutter of the shed at the farmstead where I was living and on a sunshiny day I hung in thin air . . . She jumped down and landed right on a piece of wood with rusted nails that went through the bottom of her pretty pink canvas shoe and into her sole. From now on, only the other shoe could step in the puddles.

The girl sat on the grass, untied the shoe, lifted her foot cautiously away from the nail and the shoe, and took off her socks. Although the nail had stabbed her deep, there was little blood; more came when she pinched the wound. Soffia had once taught her to put a copper coin on a wound from a rusty nail— or else you could get blood poisoning. She was just beginning to worry about blood poisoning when two gunshots resounded from the house. In response the cow lowed knowingly, and Rafael dragged the man who'd combed his hair across the door-step, by his feet, and out onto the lawn, then headed back in. He quickly returned with the other man, who was holding the letter. Perhaps he'd been trying to use it as a shield or a suit of armor. Maybe that could happen someday in the future, when words really have power.

With one foot sock-less, Billie looked up. If Rafael saw her, he avoided seeing her; he stood over the bodies of the two men, his overalls splattered, he spat on the grass, he kicked at the pave-ment with needless force—it was only, after all, pavement. "The bloody devil, the fucking fiend. I don't feel like burying these men. Fuck it, fuck it, fuck it." The rage in his voice reminded her of someone who was just about to cry. He grabbed the red gas can, splashed gasoline over the corpses, and threw a lit match on the pile as soon as the suits were soaked. It quickly became a great blaze. The corpses burst into flames and the smoke twist-ed into a blade in the sky. The grass base turned to soot. Rafael lit a cigarette, stuck it between his lips, shoveled gravel into the wheelbarrow, and tipped it from the wheelbarrow over the patch, leveling the gravel with the garden rake. "Stop staring, girl," he said, as the rake's teeth rattled through the gravel. The cow lowed. The chickens made sure they weren't heard from or seen.

"I'm not a girl."

"What are you then?"

"I'm a young maid."

Rafael laughed gruffly.

"I hurt myself, I hurt myself, I'm badly wounded, I need a copper penny, but the safe is locked."

Rafael threw a coin up into the air so it gleamed, a brownish-red penny, and it landed in her open palm. Wow, a fine copper coin, right out of a murderer's pocket. Billie pressed the metal to the wound. "I need a band-aid," she said. It was really great, she thought, empowering, to make demands. Perhaps one ought to be demanding in a murderer's presence. Rafael set the garden rake against the house wall, beside the soldier's boot, the soldier's boot and the garden rake side by side, the soldier's boot and the garden rake, the soldier's boot and the garden rake side by side, the soldier's boot and the garden rake up against the white-painted house porch; he went in and came back with a band-aid, a band-aid, a band-aid, and put it on Billie. Mmm, the smell of a fabric band-aid is really good. Marius thought fabric band-aids were better than the plastic ones. Marius knew literally everything, alt, alles, allt, todo about things from the pharmacy. The smell from a plastic band-aid wasn't bad, no need to leave it out, but this here, mmmmm—to speak plainly, this was all absurd.

Rafael fixed two band-aids in a cross on top of the copper penny, directly over the wound, and he dressed Billie in her sock before lacing her shoe tight, the way only a grown-up knows how e.g., her mom; e.g., Marius; e.g., her dad. Recitation finished. Billie put her arms around his neck, to show that he should hold her when she was injured. Rafael took her in his arms and carried her across the lawn. But he stopped at the doorway.

"You can't come in before I'm done tidying up," he said. "Some cleaning is not for kids."

He turned around and sauntered into the hen house with Billie in his arms, put her down in the corner beside the stove, which was never lit except in winter, waved to her, and left. Remarkable. To put a girl in a hen house while he was washing the floor after two killings in a war zone. What's more, the hens were offended by this apparition. Cocksure on their perches.

What is the old biddy doing in here with us? We own this house. Don't soil our house, little miss rascal.

The soldier left me here, I didn't decide anything. I have to lie here while the patches of blood are being cleaned up.

The chickens accepted the girl's answer, and they continued to let their eyelids droop as they warmed the eggs. Billie closed her eyes, too. It would be fun to go to China with her father. The two of them. To stroll along the Great Wall. It would not be too dangerous for his twisty gait—if his feet slipped, he always could hang by the puppet strings and the puppeteers would haul him back onto the wall.

Hi Dad, isn't it fun to stroll along the Great Wall of China?

Yes, it is, my li'l cruller, take in the view here and take a swig of the air, Billie. You won't find that scent anywhere but in China.

She drank the sweet, fresh scent of China, mmmmm, good scent, Dad. Should we go down and have tea with the ancient monks?

Excellent idea, Billie, excellent idea. You are a very resource-ful traveling companion.

I am a better travel companion than I am a single girl stuck at home, a homebody, a homer, a homey-buddy. I find all that boring.

Yes, my love, name what you want to be when you are big and your wishes will come true. Won't you please remember me? For I'll surely remember you, all the time and at all times, but if you need to call me, you should know I have no phone.

Billie cut her eyes sideways at the chickens, like a spy, and they glanced sideways at her, like spies. Rafael's head appeared between the wooden beams and the door:

"Do you think the princess is awake?"

She decided to wake up, to squint her eyes, the way she'd seen in movies, the way movie actresses who aren't actually asleep appear to sleep in front of the camera; she decided to stretch and Rafael extended her a hand. She rubbed the sleep from her eyes before taking his hand. Rafael massaged his aching forehead with the other. Then he led the girl back to the humans' house.

**XXV.** The white box of watercolors with the transpar-ent lid housed sixteen colors in individual circular compartments. One color was so beautiful that Billie couldn't bring herself to ever use it. Another color was so beautiful that she'd made a deep hole in it. Gold for the sun. Green for the grass. Blue and white for the sea and the sky. Brown for the earth and for things like trees. Billie moistened a paintbrush in a glass of water, rubbed it lightly in the color and painted a red box on a big white sheet; she colored the box fully because an ogre lived inside it, even though you couldn't see the ogre in the picture. Rafael drank a beer in big gulps, a soldier's beer which came out of the black crate.

"I didn't want to kill those men," he said, watching the paintbrush stretch red color across the page in gentle strokes. "This is war, and I am forced to take part in it. It's self-evident that they would have killed me if I hadn't killed them. And then what would have become of my girl?"

"Perhaps I am a girl, but I am not yours."

"I invited them inside so the animals and you didn't have to see the bloodshed. That's the reason I closed the door. Very much a summerhouse of loneliness. It was either me or them. No more complicated than that. No more complicated than that."

"Wasn't the gun inside, too?" Billie asked. "Then that was extremely clever of you. They stumbled into a trap."

"Yes, that was extremely clever of me, but I would have preferred to be without all this, and I won't accept their car as the spoils of war. Not from these men. They were not good men, Billie. They were malicious and evil."

"Aren't your enemies always evil? Spoils of war don't come from good people."

"Don't good people live here, Billie? I feel like only good people have lived in Reindeer Woods."

She drew a small ape beside the red crate.

"I am only somewhat good," she said, "my mom is good, she is the best, my dad and Marius."

"Is your mother beautiful?"

"You're not allowed to ask me that."

Rafael asked for the paintbrush and a blank page, and he settled down at the kitchen table. "Mom advised me to join the army. I would lie at home and sleep for days. She said: Rafael, do you want to become dreck and flotsam? You seem like a sensible and good boy. She said that I was an intelligent, good boy. She was agitating. Through it, she set me on the right route."

He painted a lamb with red lips. "Mom felt like she wasn't able to have a positive and uplifting effect on her son. I have failed as a mother, Rafael, you will sleep away your life if you follow me. I have been a melancholy influence on my son. You need a different mother. You need the army as a mother. Mom was right. I went into the army, learned to wake up in the morning, to think for myself, to be responsible for my body, to exercise it, and to tell right from wrong."

"Don't be mournful, soldier," said Billie, longing to be grown-up and to dry the tears from the corners of his eyes, but she wasn't grown-up, there were no tears, and she sketched a princess by the red crate. Beside the lamb, Rafael sketched a muscled man in swimming trunks.

"Billie, can you drive a car?"

"Can eleven-year-old kids drive cars?"

"Kids in the country know many things that kids in the city don't know."

"I'm not a country kid."

"My apologies, young miss."

Correct. That's how he should talk to her. Please, go ahead.

"Would you feel bad if I taught you to drive and then you drove the orange car and I the blue one? I'm keen to rid myself of that spoil of war. Those men hurt me. I won't be free until I do so."

"If I drive you to destroy the car, will I be an accessory? I don't want to be an accessory."

"This is war. You would be obeying my commands."

"Yessir, skipper," she replied, jauntily. Abraham said that to Soffia from time to time: Yessir, skipper. He meant that she was bossy, which she was, as she needed to be, living with a man who was controlled by three strangers from another planet. If she hadn't been bossy, then they would have controlled her, too, and she wouldn't have been able to tend to other people as well as Abraham. Healing a puppet is the easiest thing in the world. One only has to glue, or sew, it together. Hardly onerous work for an idealist doctor. The girl knew that. Soffia's authoritative behavior was a defense mechanism. One time, she heard her mother say into the phone:

My authoritative behavior is my personal defense mechanism.

One day, the girl would find her own personal defense mechanism. Remember that. Don't forget to discover your own personal defense mechanism. She stamped her feet.

"Why are you stamping your feet, Billie?"

"Because I'm reminding myself of something which I might otherwise forget."

"Are you writing a mental list in your head?"

"Something like that," she replied, and she sneezed. The cat was here some place, that scoundrel, it was poisoning her, but that didn't mean she would kill it. She stamped her feet again. The discomfort others cause you, whether animals or men, shouldn't be repaid with discomfort; instead, you should let it pass without reacting.

"Billie, are you scolding me or are you still stamping a mental list?"

"I'm reflecting," she answered the soldier.

"Could you pay attention to me? The war won't wait for you to finish reflecting."

"What, man? What do you want?" she screamed, screamed her individual defense mechanism.

"Calm down," answered Rafael, and he asked if she would prefer it if he aimed the gun at her when he ordered her to go to the orange car and taught her to drive it, so that she would not be considered an accessory if it turned out that the military invasion lost the game—even though it seemed there was no chance of that now. "I promise not to shoot you. Although this is war and I am a soldier with complete license from my army commander to break my word and promise, I never have and never will break the words of any promise I make myself or others."

"Your words and your promise are a solace against grief," said Billie, and she slammed down the box of colors. The infantry soldier popped out to get the weapon.

*XXVI.* "Tell me mister soldier, if I'm driving the orange car and you the blue one, what happens if I drive out in front of you and disappear into the distance."

"Then the car will blow up."

"Wow, now I'm looking forward to learning to drive," said Billie, and she went in front of Rafael, the gun barrel in her back, until they stopped at the driver's door of the orange car. He opened the door. She sat at the wheel. He sat in the passenger seat with the weapon between his thighs, put the key in the ignition, moved the driver's seat so that the girl's feet touched the pedals, pointed to the gas pedal at the same time as he tapped her right knee, pointed to the clutch at the same time as he tapped her left knee, pointed to the brake and patted her right knee again. He showed her the gear stick. He showed her how to drive and to change gears from 1 to 4, R for reverse. He ordered her to put the car in reverse and to back away from the parking spot. She did so. Then she spun away from the spot along the path up to the highway.

At the intersection, one would turn left if you were planning to go up from the valley over the Ceaseless Heath along the mountain road, and from there along the Endless Pass towards the rock face in Forever Valley, but Billie was ordered to turn right, and Reindeer Woods appeared, serene in the afternoon light, on the left hand side with pine woods covering the slope on the right. Two deer grazing in the afternoon disappeared into a glade. A fox's red tail shot past the old fence post. The little wood-birds were chased by squirrels, and the martens crept about on their feet after the day's sleep. Yellow roadside flowers had just recently closed themselves for the evening, were immoderately early-sleepers, with each decade they slept earlier and earlier.

The way the girl drove wasn't exciting; it didn't make her passenger gasp for breath. The girl knew this. The soldier stretched in his seat, with one hand on the gun shaft.

"For years I've wanted to sit in a car driven by a girl," he said.

"Then you've got your wish."

She was trying to avoid saying too much; talking too much might distract her, and she didn't feel like pulling an old jalopy out of a ditch or turning it over if it rolled.

"All the girls I dated were worse than boring. I asked them to drive my car, but they refused. I longed to lie stretched out in the passenger seat, to roll back my eyes in a hopeless dream. Indeed, one of them did. She was a bit strange. Even I couldn't be with her, though I tried. I gave her a chance. I could boast afterwards that I was the one who gave her a chance. That was a rose in my buttonhole. I am against bullying. You aren't strange, Billie."

"One of my schoolmates said I was strange. Perhaps I am strange."

"This schoolmate of yours might himself have been strange."

"He was a little strange."

"You are the least strange girl I know, Billie. I wish one of those girls had been like you."

"Would you have married her?" Billie asked, curiously.

"I don't know whether I trust myself to marry. Perhaps I'm not an eligible husband. Women frighten me. I wish I'd met a girl like you. Or someone who was like Maria was for Marius. Or like your mother when your father came to the emergency room. Some honey, with an aftertaste. The girls who I met were all the same."

"You've just licked the surface," said Billie; she'd first heard that sentence either in a movie or from her mother's lips when she'd been talking into the phone.

Rafael pointed to the turn-off on the road as he said, "That's true. I've only licked the surface."

Billie headed along the rough path, which ended at the old sheep house, turned around, then drove the car the short way back home, pulling up in front of the white-painted garden gate. The children in Reindeer Woods welcome us. Rafael didn't need to fear a kamikaze crash from the girl. He ordered her to step out of the vehicle and stand by the garage while he went inside. He came back out of the garage with an army backpack.

"Here is a bomb," he said. "Do you want to feel how heavy

a bomb is? It's so heavy you wouldn't be able to lift it. No, you can't feel it." He took the bomb, which reminded her of a battery, out of the backpack and placed it on the back seat of the orange car. "In sixty minutes it's going to explode." He showed the girl a little tool that he also got out of the backpack. "This is the remote. If something isn't right, I can push this switch and the car will explode into the air. Get in the car and drive off once I beep. We'll head down the valley to the water."

"Since you're planning to destroy it, why don't you let me drive the blue car? If I get into an accident and the orange car explodes, you'll be forced to drive the blue one for ever after."

Rafael massaged his forehead.

"This damn headache. I can't think for this headache. Me, who's always longed to be a farmer. I love animals. Why do I get this headache now when everything is just getting going? Do I need some sugar? Orange juice? Tomorrow I will have some orange juice. There are at least three orange trees in the garden. Vegetables, I will eat more vegetables. Perhaps it has something to do with my eyes, but I'm not having trouble with my sight. Maybe it would be good to pierce my ears. Are soldiers allowed to have earrings on the battlefield? I want to grow a beard. In winter, I'll grow a beard. Then I'll have stopped being a soldier. And stopped smoking. I don't want to get lung cancer. Does it get cold here in winter?"

He was murmuring nothing but nonsense, but who doesn't under pressure? Then he aimed the gun at Billie:

"No. Children can't drive the spoils of war. Start the orange car."

Billie did. When the blue car honked she shot the car so sharply from its spot that the bomb in the back seat slid around.

"Hush, little bomb. You aren't allowed to explode while I am in the car because then my mom would suffer. She longed to have a girl exactly like me, and it would be a shame if the girl died."

At the intersection with the highway, she turned the car to the right.

*xxvii.* The shadows from the mountain moved across the road and fell over a third of the valley, but they didn't reach the farmstead, the hayfield, or the moor on the far side, where the easterly slopes were bathed in horizontal rays of afternoon sun. The cow lowed and the chickens pecked at the gravel, glancing towards the highway and watching the orange car run down towards the bottom of the valley, the blue one some distance behind it, but when white smoke swirled up from the orange hood and hid the rest of the car, they didn't feel like watching any more. The headlights of the blue car flashed and the horn honked, but Billie wasn't paying attention; she was determined to hold tight to the heavy steering wheel as car accelerated down the slope and she decided to lightly press her shoe against the brake. With that the car danced and the steering wheel moved of its own accord, stones and rocks spun up onto the hood. She thought she was driving into a fog. Better to step on the brake harder. All the way down. The monster pulled up, her head dashed against the steering wheel and it began to swell. Rafael opened the door, said something about how the driver had done fine on her maiden voyage, opened the hood, and disappeared into the white smoke.

"The tank is out of water."

Like Billie cared about an empty tank. She massaged the bump on her forehead. "The tank is out of water," he repeated. When road movies took you inside traveling cars, it was a matter of principle that the radio should be on—and Billie was a genuine traveler. Soffia knew that: It's rare that you find such a good travel companion as our Billie. Our girl is a born wanderer, she said to Abraham, who wasn't forbidden from traveling with them, but who chose to sit at home, toothless, rather than traveling without teeth. He was waiting for things to change. And also, and also, he explained before Soffia bought the airplane tickets, I have to finish the jurisprudence book first. When I have teeth, when I have written the book of laws, then I'll let myself travel.

Soffia established a secret fund, a reserve fund, a collection fund, a bank account under the name: My friend's teeth. Does one abandon someone who cannot smile? They were words from an old movie. No, first give them teeth. Then abandon them. It wasn't always child's play to be self-sacrificing, or virtuous, e.g., Abraham, who became very jealous over Soffia's comments about their daughter's natural-born wanderlust, and so he invited his daughter to go somewhere with him when they could, just the two of them. The three of them dreamed of the Taj Mahal and Alcatraz, but there were plenty of other options. Billie and Abraham go to Africa. Billie and Abraham in the Antarctic. Penguins welcome the two of them. Billie and Abraham visit the Alps. Billie and Abraham in Florida. Billie fiddled with the dial on the radio and stopped at a deep radio voice:

"This is a strange war. The victims are hard to make out. We don't know how many have died. We don't know how many soldiers from the invasion force are in the country. We know little but feel ever more fear, we are despairing and humiliated.

Goods and resources disappear. In the evenings and at night everything is murky and quiet. We wait in fear for bombing raids. The government works secretly. It promises to look out for our concerns and for its citizens' belongings. It is sending the message that people should not give up now."

"What are you listening to?" asked Rafael, and he stood over the open car door. "Please turn off the radio."

"Can't I do anything?"

"No, you're a prisoner of war, prisoners of war don't listen to the radio and amuse themselves in the driver's seat while their captors toil and slave away. Don't you understand the rules? Where were you born, kid? Understand reality, young lady."

Reality. Realidad. Raunveruleiki. Virkeligheten. Genjitsu. She neither listened to nor watched the soldier as he poured water into the reservoir. Just changed the channel, beginning to lose interest in staring at the muscled body, broad neck, ears as small as an eleven year-old girl's, as hairy as a young mouse. Her shoulders shook in time with a rock song: Maria come home. I'm tired of hanging out here alone. Come home quick, quick, quick. Remember what fun we had last summer. Last summer, last summer, last summer.

Rafael slammed the hood down, bent over the door, and said:

"There's twenty five minutes left on the bomb, lady. Start up the car, turn it in the direction of the road, and drive until we come to the water."

With a flick of his hand, he turned off the radio and gave Billie a smack on the back of her neck.

"Damn, ouch! Dick-head."

"Lady, no one talks to me like that. Doesn't anything get into your thick skull?"

Recalling the fifth article of the declaration of human rights—no one shall suffer either torture or cruel, inhuman, or disrespectful treatment or punishment—she reached out for the car door, but Rafael got the better of her and slammed the door in the girl's face. She started the car, drove it onto the road in the right direction, headed to the water, stopped the car at a well-tended parking place made of a vibrantly-colored red gravel, and hobbled out. The sun stood at the mountain's edge like a crown and glittered on the water's surface. Short bushes grew in illogical directions around the sandy banks. It was still, but different than the quiet farmstead, perhaps like being in a sky-sized leather bag, though without the claustrophobia. A few birds sung lullabies. Others called to each other: Come back home, whimbrel. Come, white wagtail, marybird, I'm starting to miss you. Come, redwing, we can't start without you. The little hotheads flying about up in the wispy veils of cloud stopped a while to consider the human intrusion on their place, feeling out this novelty, uncertain about how best to react. Hands in pockets, hands in jeans pockets, a slim pink belt, a slim pink belt. She prodded about in the gravel with her favorite footwear, sat down Indian-style and in yoga poses until the blue car arrived, parking at a deliberate distance from the orange one, which hadn't missed it one bit.

*XXVIII.* Rafael carried the bomb from the orange car and put it between the front seats of the blue one, like the cake the two of them had forgotten to buy at the bakery. Then he opened the trunk of the blue car.

"Come and look, Billie," he said, and Billie clambered to her feet and kicked a red stone. In the trunk was a wine-red brief-case that was filled with bank notes. The bills were new and they smelled like money. For a moment reality fused with the movies. Which came first, the chickens or the eggs, and who would believe her when she began:

The day was well on its way to night when I saw the brief-case in the trunk of a blue automobile. It was full of bills. It was like the things you see in movies, but in the emotional turmoil I must admit I came to and asked myself: Billie, are you an opportunist?

Poor Soffia, who was utterly against opportunists, had with great pain and labor given birth to one, an opportunist, some-one who she would also eventually find out was retarded.

"They cleaned out farmers to get this. Customs agents are going around the region, robbing folk by honest means, not dis-honestly, as the army is accused of doing. Does it matter who you pay your taxes to? The ones who used to rule the country or us? Doesn't matter. Doesn't matter. Doesn't matter. It's all the same tobacco, Billie. I regret it, but that's how it is. I am no better than them. They are no better than me," said Rafael, slamming the case closed. According to him, opportunism was a normal life-choice, and it was beyond criticism. He took some black sunglasses and a fire extinguisher from the trunk and threw them onto the ground, but Billie picked up the sunglasses and set them loosely on her nose. Rafael threw the briefcase on the back seat of the blue car and said he wouldn't accept bribe money or take part in this debauchery, "I want to be clean," he said.

"You are clean," said Billie, and she looked at his well-washed hair, so clean that his mother and father could be proud to have him for a son. There was no dirt, not even a trace, and no sign of disregard for his own body.

"I will rinse myself of this war. I won't behave like the majority."

"The majority rules in a democracy," said Billie wildly, eager to take part in a constructive conversation, trying to be a competent conversationalist, as her mother called it. You are not a competent conversationalist, fella, she'd heard Soffia tell Abraham after a whole night spent debating, planning the future. You are just not conversation competent, Soffia repeated, and she went into the kitchen, put the coffee on, and shouted from the kitchen: You need to wake the child. Our child needs to go to school, or were you about to forget? Perhaps he was about to forget. Abraham could forget that the weeks and days passed.

"And the majority of people are greedy," said Rafael, who locked all the doors and the trunk on the blue car, like that mattered for a car which was about to explode.

"May I have the sunglasses?" she asked, and she was amazed by his unaffected yes and the absence of any further comeback. That was relaxing. She recovered her interest in Rafael, she was just as forgetful as her dad, forgetting that here was an opportunist and murderer. Who wanted to be a better man. Shouldn't one give people another chance? And she was an opportunist. Would grab opportunity while it was there. Give the man another chance. According to the red wristwatch on her wrist, the second-hand was only a ninety-degree angle away from when the bomb would explode. In an instant she ran to shelter behind the orange car. Was it the soldier's plan to blow her up too? She didn't want to die. Now she was sure of that. Who wants that?

Some. You see, my Billie, how some people live their own lives. Isn't their lifestyle often marked by a longing to die, a longing to shorten their way, to speed their trip through this life? Why do they want that? the thin, eccentric asked the child.

I don't know, Dad.

I don't know either, replied Abraham, scratching the backs of his ears.

"Were you going to blow me up, leave me behind with the blue car?" she asked, gasping. "Why did you leave me behind? I was attending to my duties as prisoner of war, one hundred percent."

"Relax," he said, holding the remote, "everything's under control."

Billie peeked around the orange car and looked at her red wristwatch.

"It hasn't blown up. Why didn't it blow up? According to my clock sixty minutes has passed."

"Do you want to push the button?" he asked, showing her the remote. "Every kid likes to push the button."

"Not me."

Rafael looked at the blue car one last time, then he took the girl's head and hid it between his arms. She could barely hold her breath, but the smell of the blue turtleneck sweater was good. A blend of ape and carpet. Though she had never smelled an ape, never been to the zoo. Why didn't her parents take her to the zoo? Abraham and Soffia simultaneously:

"Billie dear, we don't want to show you animals in captivity."

What about the chickens on the farm? Weren't they prisoners? Whether a man is a chained-up prisoner or not is a matter of degree. A specimen, not a specimen. A complicated example.

Different levels of quality in prisoners. Rafael pressed the button. A thud came from the earth as the bomb exploded, and a bellow of thunder threw them up off the ground—they landed three or four meters from the orange car. The explosion resounded around the valley. After that there was a deep silence, broken only by a far-off lowing, an unexpected barking. They inched themselves around the orange car. Billie took off the sunglasses. Thin black smoke rose to the sky. Crumpled together bits of iron the length of a rifle lay on the ground. Around these bits played flames which inclined their tips to the gods and then burned out. As though through witchcraft, in no time at all, things had disappeared from reality. She put on the sunglasses. They were a dead man's sunglasses, but she didn't care—who wasn't dead nowadays.

"I want to smoke," she said. Since she'd started driving cars, why not smoke? "Gimme a smoke," she said to Rafael, who got the cigarette packet from his pocket.

"The good thing about the army is that it provides you with smokes; it bribes you with tobacco, money, medicine, and a pension. A reliable return when one grows old. For the soldier and his spouse."

"That is, friend, if you win the war."

"We'll win it. We are just about to win it."

"Well then. Since you say that."

He lit her cigarette. She breathed out. That was fun: looking at the empty stain where the car had been parked five minutes earlier and smoking. Fantastic fun.

This summer was the summer I learned to drive a car, saw a car blow up in a parking spot, and began to smoke.

"Come on."

Rafael retrieved the luggage from the trunk of the orange car. Then they left with the fishing rod, the tent, the sleeping bags, and the other important accessories which are associated with going camping.

**XXIX.** This region of the planet disappeared into shadows as they traveled to face the darkness of outer space. Soon the stars glittered and the moon appeared, the puppet of the earth, the earth its puppet; controlling woman's monthly cycles and the tides, it must affect many other things as well. And so it happened that Billie traveled after all, though she didn't travel far; meanwhile Abraham and Soffia were far away, missing all the fun, as people say about minor events. Billie and Rafael lay in sleeping bags; hers was light blue on the outside, dark blue on the inside, his was black on the outside, orange on the inside. At the edge of the tent a fire burned, and Billie prodded it with a slender tree branch. Flakes of fires floated up from it, burning bright and dying quickly, while Rafael smoked and refused to give her a drag or another cigarette. He was pretending that he was looking after her, but it was just stinginess, just stinginess, he'd had enough of debauchery, now he wanted Billie, like him, to become what he called "clean," whatever that meant. She reckoned it was part of some secret code grown-ups knew.

"You will only smoke one cigarette in my care," he said, and he produced two cans of beer from the green duffel bag, handing her one, "and you'll drink a single beer, no more, in my care."

She pulled her sunglasses down from her nose:

"Are you making up for your misdeeds with your rules and limits?" she asked. What fun to string words together outdoors under the bare sky. She took a gulp of beer and burped.

"I've done many bad things, countless," answered Rafael, "and if I started making up for them, they'd would certainly not go away."

"Like with the stars in the heavens. If one goes out, there's a million, a trillion left."

"I've gotten tired of killing, Billie. Killing gives me headaches. I really don't want to dig any more graves, or to hide any more bodies. That's not my job as a soldier. Next time someone comes to visit, I'll have to find another way to get rid of them."

"Wouldn't those people have killed you if you hadn't killed them, and then killed me, too, or sent me to an orphanage?"

"I can't talk about it anymore. Now we'll solemnly promise to be better people."

"Those who improve themselves are the most worthy," quoted Billie, gnawing on the ends of the sunglasses.

"You stop smoking," Rafael said to her as though she'd taken it up, "and I'll stop killing. We'll become better people. Those who improve themselves are the most worthy."

"Ain't that the truth, skipper."

Each prodded at the fire with their own branch. Done-in from its day's work drinking in the light, the vegetation caught its breath and exhaled a pleasant fragrance of leaves, flowers, moss, and heather before it sucked in the moisture evaporating from the soil. The countless stars cast down strings with fishhooks right at their very ends and hauled a few fish up, a few souls, hooked around their rear ends, up up up. Some tugged on the lines and wrapped them around their necks or other people's necks. The birds were sleeping. A four-legged animal ran at a canter and rustled the blades of grass. Martens sped along the water's surface like swimming knives. Nothing hummed from lampposts or telecommunications masts. Billie couldn't belch any more, though she really wanted to; she was a little queasy, but that was okay, the same humidity that nourished the vegetation before it slept would soothe and calm her bloated stomach. It was a fine idea to wake up somewhere other than in the bunk beside the orange chest of drawers and the red closet, a mattress on the floor in front of her.

"In the morning we'll swim, then we'll catch fish. I've learned on my travels around the country that nowhere has more beautiful lakes than here."

"I've never seen an ugly lake," said Billie, the wise traveler, the eager traveler, the best-ever travel companion.

**XXX.** Rafael got undressed quickly and systematically. Perhaps he'd learned to do that in the army. His buttocks resembled two basketball halves. They were girlish and pert as he waded out into the water. Billie got out of her denim clothes, folded them, and placed them in the reeds. She put the copper penny and the band-aid on top of the clothes. Her navel protruded like a bullet. Her mother believed that the navel would retreat when Billie entered puberty, when the egg in the ovary wanted to be impregnated. Then the ovaries would haul the navel and the umbilical cord in so they could later cast the cord out from the womb with a new shoot hanging on it. But until then her navel would push out because it was still invisibly tied to its headquarters, Soffia the wise sage. If her mother should die there would not be any knowledge left in the world.

Billie limped over to the water and stepped into the mud, which was soft on her injured foot. Goose-pimples appeared and then vanished, goose-bubbles.

She waded out, lay down in the water once it reached to her breast, and swam away from Rafael—she wanted to be free and alone, wanted to see her reflection on the surface split under her swimming strokes, the sun glinting on particles of water. She listened to the splash of her hands, whistling through the air, and birdsong. Felt the water careful and gentle on her fingers. Without knowing her, the water was kind to her. Didn't ask for her name, who her parents were, when and where she was born. It accepted her like snowflakes from the sky. Billie swam to a little waterfall which was still in the shadows cast by the morning sun. She turned around, swam back. The sun climbed the earth warm degree by warm degree. Perhaps the sun rose higher up the ladder today than the day before. Usually at this time of the morning it was hurrying its first steps up in the sky, like a girl in a fairy tale hurrying to a ball.

Billie got out of the water and went over to the grass. The goose-bubbles came back in their millions, the hairs on her arms rose. The sun dried her while her teeth chattered in her mouth. Surely it was better to bathe in a bathtub, close to a comforter or a radiator, in case you got cold afterwards. Better not to be whimsical, better to bathe at home. Why go elsewhere when there was enough water in the house, the same water as elsewhere?

Rafael's head shot up from his dive and shook at a one thousand kilometers per hour and drops of water crashed in every direction. He got out, hunched down on the dry ground, grabbed the white t-shirt, faced the other way, and hurried into his army pants, army socks, army shirt, army shoes, and his blue turtle-neck sweater (also a gift from the army). It was good that they clothed him, he didn't have to go to town and choose things himself, get everything at once from socks to underwear, over-coat and outerwear, gloves and caps, and what's more, a sleeping bag, a wallet, a lighter, his own inscribed diary, a black ballpoint pen with *ubi bene, ibi patria* in gold lettering, binoculars, a gas mask, a shaving kit, a toothbrush, a shoe horn, a needle and twine, a comb. Rafael sat on the grass beside Billie.

"You're cold," he said, "Put your clothes on."

"One shouldn't get dressed wet."

"You must put your clothes on. It's not warm out yet."

She couldn't answer through her chattering teeth. He tried to dress her, but her body was heavy and stiff, not at all compliant. So he threw her clothes over her shoulders, took the paralyzed Billie in his arms, and carried her to the car, where he put her on the back seat. She asked after the sunglasses, which he fetched, as well as a blanket which smelled of gasoline and grass. It was a thick, gray, scratchy woolen blanket, the kind the soldiers had hanging from their backpacks when they came to the farm one lunchtime a few weeks ago. Billie lay in the infamous and life-saving fetal position. She was definitely definitely definitely definitely definitely going to throw up. The automobile set off from the place. Fart fart. White fart cushions slipped from the exhaust pipe and clouded out in the air. The chickens heard the hiccup back home on the farm. One stepped out from the hen house and watched the orange automobile as it clambered back along the road.

*xxxi.* Billie saw a large spoon. Pink liquid in the spoon. From behind the spoon stared the cross-eyed Rafael. She wasn't dead. Was she dead? Involuntarily, she opened her mouth, as you do when you're presented with a spoonful of medicine. First you open your eyes, then see the spoon, then open your mouth. The spoon found its way to her mouth, the medicine ran down into her stomach. That was good. Another spoon with a white mountain of rice. "Now comes the thick soup," said Rafael, wearing his white t-shirt with his bulging arms, his green army pants, the hair on the lower parts of his fingers. Outside she heard birds, and when she glanced her eyes over to the window—surprisingly painful to move them, cardboard eyes cardboard eyes, perhaps she was already a puppet—she saw the birds fly, yellow, around the sky. She must be in a high castle tower. The light of the sky was bluer than usual, there were no glass panes visible between her and the sky, just like tower bedroom windows in an animated movie about the old days, where people could easily stick a hand right out into the fresh air. Could sample the air with their hands before sticking out their necks, before perhaps sticking their whole body out and flying down to earth. Boom. Oof, that was quite a blow. Back up again. She was a princess. Her home was up in a tower. A soldier guarded her. Soon a white dove would come and alight on the windowsill with an important letter.

*xxxii.* The curtains were drawn, and they stirred a little because of the open window on the other side of the material. A stool stood beside the bunk. Some cloth napkins were on top of the stool next to a water glass and a few pieces of apple. A clean towel was spread over her pillow. Rafael lay on the floor in the farmer's nightshirt, one of his feet on top of the blanket. Perhaps it was possible to unscrew it, perhaps it wasn't possible to unscrew it. Billie took a few sips of water then lay back, looking up into the air, at the underside of the upper bunk. There were drawings, writing. She turned on the night lamp quietly and read: You kangaroo-pig. You fit in my pouch. Dick-head. Donkey brain. Chameleon. Pongy toes. Do you have asthma? Skip-and-swing. Sexmaniac. Fart fart. Chewing gum machine. My heart is a kite and I can't tug it to earth. Sing hallelujah. You boaster. Ass. Turd. Billie + Marius ≠ false love. You're a pompous ass. Pipecleaner. Soup-pot. Cinnamon heart. A picture of a heart. A picture of an ice-cream in a cone. A picture of a crown. She turned off the light. Rafael stirred and said: "Obviously I could ski down the peak." Speaking in his dream. Billie lay on her side, wrapped the comforter around her tighter, closed her eyes, and searched for the right thought, the one which would drift her to sleep rather than keep her wakeful.

*xxxiii.* Right before the official start of the day, she went outside in her nightdress. The grass was damp from night. The tent hung on the laundry line. The chickens were resting inside the hen house. The roosters gaped absent-mindedly at this being: Was it a new delegate of the heavenly smiths or of the farmer? But in all likelihood they'd simply never seen a nightdress with pictures of mermaids. Behind the house the cow rose to its feet after the night's rest and also stared at her, but with mournful eyes that protruded like a girl's navel. She wiped the sleep from the corners of the cow's eyes and embraced the cow, cheek to cheek. Aww, aww, what if the cow was tired of being a cow? Is the world perhaps tired of being the world just before it gets going at this first hour of the morning? Then the cow lowed and excited the roosters, which crowed into the emptiness. Then the cow answered and the chickens appeared from their nesting place, waddled out from the cabin to see what was up, tripped behind the house wearing nature's nightdresses (or at least with a veil of night about them) and saw the girl accompanying the cow down to the lot. They stared after the female friends the way only chickens do. The girl freely took the cow's tail. They led each other that way like girlfriends.

On the way into the lower garden she knelt down beside the lake and rested her chin on the mossy bank. The goldfish slept. Fish food—yellow, green, and brown flakes—floated in the water. The coins that had belonged to the two men who had once sat in the white chairs by moonlight lay out of reach on the bottom. One of them had emptied his jeans pocket:

In the hope that our wishes in regards to this matter come true, namely that the whole of humankind pulls itself together and stops all the swindling. No matter how contemptible or grave the swindling is, it's all the same. Abolish swindling from the world and try to live without it from then on. It doesn't have to be difficult. Let's not avoid inconveniences, let's not take shortcuts by swindling. Never steal from others to gain yourself. Let's concentrate on more personal pronouns than just the first person singular. May the government make a speech which begins: We propose that we should all stop swindling, as one. Those were the first man's words. Then the other man emptied his pockets into the water:

We won't stop smoking, but we will stop swindling. We'll stop telling lies and stop thinking along conventional lines, with every cliché competing with other clichés for space in one's brain. First and foremost, I will stop thinking about my own interests. I will think just as beautifully about my body as about plants in the greenhouse, and I'll respect my thoughts. My thoughts are full of squabbles. I intend to stop bickering about those squabbles before I stop smoking. Before I stop smoking, said the man, stamping his feet in turn a few times in the grass as confirmation of his promise. Then they sat back in the chairs and continued talking together in low voices. The men's wishes will one day be fulfilled, since it's nature's desire to fulfill things, and then the whole world would stop swindling. The girl stuck her hand down in the water and the fish woke from their tranquil nap.

*xxxiv.* "Hey, my chickens," she said, stroking the loose combs of a few chickens as she went past the staring chicks. A gunshot reverberated from the house. The chickens followed the girl inside, though no further into the living room than a bashful girlfriend would have allowed herself; restrained, well-mannered, and on their best behavior, they loved the smell of the newly-organized interior and because of this they got a nice pang in their hen-bellies, which appeared to human eyes as a gentle wiggle. Life was good, even though it was bad. Billie set the kitchen stool in front of the kitchen stove. Rafael limped down the stairs in his nightshirt. "Hey, my chickens," he said. He was bleeding from the toes on one foot. "A repentant man's morning work," he explained to Billie, who was standing on the stool and making coffee. He opened his palm and showed her his shot-off toe before he put it in the trash. "You're busy making coffee, my dear," he said once he had closed the cupboard where the trash was kept.

"And you're busy shooting your toe, my dear," she said; she took the funnel from the coffee flask, set it in the sink, screwed the lid on the flask, and handed it to the man.

"I'm done with murder weapons," he said, pouring coffee into a cup. Billie clambered down from the stool. She dusted the last grains from the malt cocoa tin into a glass she filled with milk. "Just now I packed the guns away and made a serious deal with myself. The toes in the trash deserved murdering because of the past. In the future I will shoot off one toe for each person who gets transformed into a corpse on my account. Whether or not that's out of self-defense." At the same time, he got some new headache pills from the black case which came by airplane and swallowed two with coffee. "That's saintly coffee," he said.

"And the best pain medicine in the world today. The army knows how to do that," she said, repeating his earlier words.

"Now our work awaits us. Feeding the chickens, fetching the eggs, milking the cow, weeding the plant beds."

"Awaits you," she corrected him, "I'm still a child."

"The carrots should be ready, according to the vegetable book I read yesterday. One of the most fascinating books I've ever read. For lunch we could have some fresh spinach straight from the garden, some carrots, and eggs. Agreed?"

"Agreed."

They high-fived each other.

"What would you say to raising rabbits? Then we could eat rabbit meat and sew rabbit gloves. Perhaps I could teach you to shoot. Then we could catch ourselves some excellent bird meat for dinner."

"The soldier forgets I'm a kid. According to the United Nations' international children's treaty, I'm prohibited from laboring away."

"You're a shrewd girl."

"Perhaps retarded."

"It's safer if I teach you to shoot in case I need your help one day. If you learn to do it once, then you know it for the rest of your life. You could go hunting with your mother when the war is over. So let's look for rabbits in the valley and cultivate rabbits. I am going to sew some rabbit-skin gloves for you. Wonderfully elegant."

She was getting practice in contradictions. Hanging the chicken and mourning the murdered dog. Packing away the weapons and unpacking them on the same day because they'd found a new purpose—procuring food instead of the things that brought on the headaches, maybe even brain-damage, resulting in others' deaths. When does one have permission to kill others? How many need to stand behind a single murderer in order for him to kill justly? One thousand men, one million, three million? If the majority rules, can the majority also kill? In Abraham's book of laws one might read:

> Those who commit murder and have no one but themselves in their corner are thrown in prison when their killing comes to light. Those who murder and have the government on their side are not thrown in prison. The outcomes are almost identical. In both cases, the world's population has decreased by one, but one murdered is

guilty, and the other is not guilty. Every person is valuable. Each and every single person is sacred. In war, the murders committed by the victors are unimpeachable—the same way as the insane are not held responsible for their crimes. People flock to the victory feast at the public asylum, fun fun, fireworks are directed into the sky, fun fun, sailors dance with girls, old women dance with politicians, old men blow their noses heroically, young people cook food, and children get to stay up late.

*XXXV.* Billie would accompany Rafael on his usual morning route, but she wouldn't exert herself unless she was in the mood. "One also needs to show others respect, even during war," she said to Rafael, who was a civilized soldier, not a pure-bred slave driver with a whip. One morning when the breeze played about his young cheeks, this sentence was echoing around his head as he turned over the plant bed. With waders on his feet and one palm on the pitchfork handle, he loosened the ground, threw the first forkful behind him, turned the earth over, and his mouth repeated: "One also needs to show others respect, even during war," again and again. As he repeated it, his headache disappeared. Apart from certain individual fits, the worst ones, Rafael managed his aching head with the bare minimum of pain medication and by repeating sentences like: *One also needs to show others respect, even during* war. *Each person has to go and thread her own crow-path. Giving is another way of loving. The heart fills the sail with air. The number of fatalities is unknown. Justice is a goddess. If you want something you can achieve it. Soon better times will come, there'll be flowers in the meadow. The well of wisdom never runs dry. I am alone but I am not lonely. I must stop wearing a mask.* Hopefully the supply of pain medication from the army won't dry up. Hopefully neither Rafael nor Billie would become mute.

Getting the freshly-laid eggs was the first task each morning. Billie stood inside the door of the hen house and held the string that turned the light on and off; she also held the egg basket into which Rafael placed the eggs. His head reached up to the rafters, and feathers and sawdust got tangled in his hair, which grew longer than even a soldier engaged in peaceful activities could consider fitting. Billie didn't boast out loud about her pink baseball cap, Marius's baseball cap, but the cap would forever be an invincible defense against getting lice. She went into the kitchen very carefully with the egg basket, holding the palm of one hand underneath the bottom of the basket, imagining the way a midwife holds a new-born wrapped in a big diaper.

Then they would go down to the garden. Billie held the empty bucket. Rafael sat on a log by the cow, stroked her belly, and said, "Hey cow, the milk maid has come to milk you, pal." The bovine lowed in gratitude and swung her tail in a friendly way. It was good to unburden herself of each day's extra weight. The girl handed him the bucket, which he propped in the grass underneath the udders; he tugged up and down on an udder until milk ran out from the channel. Often she fed the cow grass—it could be good to munch something while you were being milked. How remarkable that food should grow at the cow's feet. It came to her, right to her front door, and never anything but green, so how remarkable, remarkable that it emerged from her breast as white milk. An internal machine whipped green grass into white milk. The magic behind the reality promised something even more remarkable still, something that surpassed the powers of the imagination. In the trouser pocket of the farmer's bib overalls was a tin of udder balm. Every three or four days they put Vaseline on the udders and she eased the sleep from the cow's eyes with a handkerchief, but the cow was sad at that time every other day.

One morning when Rafael was sitting on the log doing the milking and Billie was holding blades of grass up to the cow's mouth, a dove flew into the garden and briefly alighted on the back of the cow, gray and white with a pink beak and pink shoes, as though she had bought some lipstick and the shoes at the same store; this was certainly an out-going, social little dove. Then she shat on the cow, raised her wings, and flew off. The farmer was inclined to chase the dove with a gun, this dove that was swimming through the air, if you could say the air was made of water, but it disappeared from the valley at lightning speed. The cow lowed. Mooooo. Billie stuffed more blades into its mouth. Rafael fetched a rag. In the middle of the waste he found a red necklace and pendant, rinsed it under the water, and gave it to Billie; it was the third gift she'd got from a man. First she'd gotten a smile. The second: chocolate. Everything comes in threes, and she breathed relief, no more gifts would come from this direction.

"I am never going to fall in love," she said as he tied the necklace around her neck.

"Love is for teenagers, said Marius, don't you remember, and that means you will meet it later, but fortunately I'm no longer a teenager."

"You have just escaped the major danger."

"Yes," replied Rafael, solemnly.

"I will defend against it like a monster, it is a monster. If some boy comes and asks me to go with him, I will fart at him."

"It's a lucky guy who'll get you."

"Don't say that so gleefully, fella."

It was delightful to make conversation under the bare sky around the trees and amid the strong scent of grass, to take a break from farm work and have a necklace fastened around one's neck which had appeared in the bird shit of a city dove that was passing through.

"That manuscript of legal theories you talked about, that your father was writing. Was it ever published?"

They lay there in the grass under the garden wall, chewing blades of grass. The outdoor air was saving them from claustrophobia.

"Dad was preparing a study of the legal situation of people on earth, for the planet the puppeteers live on. When they tug him up, he'll need to have the book of laws in his baggage, or else he'll land on the planet and be in debt. Because of that he was always careful not to lose the manuscript. But he can also tell them various things about life on earth. He sketched down his thoughts so he could recount them when the time came."

"Why does this planet have a legal interest in earth? Does it plan to conquer us?"

"I don't know."

"I want to read your father's law book. If it's as fascinating as the vegetable book."

"The book is not meant for earth-dwellers."

"Where is it?"

"Dad has gone up to the planet with it, if they've already tugged him up. Which they will do as soon as he's finished his mission on earth."

After the milk was brought into the house, they put on their waders, which awaited them on the stone slab beside the greenhouse, and they looked in on the vegetable garden. Vegetables are sun-lovers and want warmth. The bed sloped towards the south; strips of barley and oats formed a lasting shelter in this, the hottest patch in the garden. Rafael scattered manure and assorted tinctures over the bed in a struggle against weeds. He called this "depression medication for vegetable-growing," since, he explained, "depression is like weeds around the spirit." Then he moved the low protective walls around the green allotment, and picked vegetables. Billie sometimes watered the bed with the yellow watering can and sometimes with the garden hose, giving the farmer a helping hand between playing around in empty beds or crawling under the shrubs in an unfathomable game no one else would ever get to the bottom of.

Then they had to look in on the growth inside the greenhouse, collect the cow's shit from the grass, and take part of it to the composter, the rest went directly onto the rhubarb and cabbage bed. Then up the ladder to pick plums, apples, and pears from the trees. Sweep the sidewalk. Patch things up. Paint the trellis. Mow the lawn. Rake the grass. Pick flowers and put them in the jug on the kitchen table. Pick flowers and put them in a jug on the pebbledash table out in the yard. Pick berries and practice making jam. There was plenty to do. Rafael built a rabbit cage and a second, smaller one for mice. On the tussocky ground further down from the lot, they set up rabbit bait and mousetraps which they checked every few days. In another spot they stacked the empty beer cans up on a broken-down fencepost and practiced shooting until they had to consider rationing ammunition. For safety reasons, they couldn't use up the powder and ammunition.

"How do you think it feels for a guitar-player to play on a stringless guitar?" asked Rafael one time, as they stood a few meters away from the beer cans on the fence post; he took aim. Billie held a box full of shot cartridges straight out in front of her and watched as the bullets drilled into the cans.

"Definitely boring, dog dull," she replied, jumping up and gathering the dead cans to set them together in a stack.

"If a guitar player is in an orchestra, he comes to a concert with a stringless guitar," Rafael added argumentatively, digging his hand into the case of shot cartridges which she held out. "No, that would not be fun for our miserable guitar player. He would feel shame, worthlessness, and self-disgrace around the other orchestra members and society as a whole."

"Can't guitar-strings be found for him anywhere?"

"No, nowhere, nowhere. Let's say that one day the world will run out of guitar strings."

"Yes," said Billie, and she stacked newly empty beer cans up on the post. Rafael pushed an unused shot cartridge into the chamber.

"A soldier who only practices shooting," he said, "and never proves himself in reality suffers like a guitar player with an entirely stringless guitar at a rock concert."

"Meanwhile, he only plays the guitar in a dream world," said Billie, and she pointed at her head in the same way that people pretend they've been shot in the head with a gun.

"Meanwhile, he only plays the guitar in a dream world," he mimicked, taking aim, "Meanwhile, as he only plays the guitar in a dream world," he repeated, "Meanwhile, as he only plays the guitar in a dream world."

"Nothing resembles music there," she said.

"Nothing resembles music there," he said. "To live is to give. To give is to allow others to enjoy the fruits of one's work and deeds. To kill is to put oneself in the shoes of the gods. To be human is wonderful. It is while it lasts."

He discharged the bullet at the cans, which split up from the post in a glimmering dance, skip, and crash. Billie ran around and gathered the dead cans from the grass and put them together in a stack. The stringless soldier opened the gun with style. Little raindrops ran down from the clouds at the same time as shoots of sun plunged through them; haze rose from the fence posts and the tar-paper on the shed roof. It also rose from the gun-barrel while drips ran from each of Rafael's nostrils. Billie stretched out in the grass and imagined she was the earth. She opened her mouth, closed her eyes. Opened her eyes, closed her mouth—splash, a drop parted her lips. She gave her body over to the rain and the sun and concentrated on perceiving the earth's movements. Rafael stacked up some new cans:

"Come on Billie. You have a go now."

She hardly felt like standing up—it was fun to disappear down in the grass as the rain and sun both plucked it at the same time—but out of obligation she took her shooting lesson, so that she could later talk about the subject, clear her throat, hm, hm, and say:

Well, yes, no, no, a great shame, yes yes, what shall I say, how best to begin, exactly, exactly, exactly, no no no no no, I don't mean to intimidate you with this or belittle your life experience and knowledge and training and wisdom when I say that I have completed the first stage of target practice. My teacher was a surrendered . . . no, he wasn't a surrendered soldier, he was a stringless guitar player, a soldier without an army, no, he was a soldier who had voluntarily taken a decision to stop killing people. Yes, or a soldier who discharged the office of governor in the valley where I was based. A soldier who didn't know whether he was a present soldier or former or a farmer. Yes, yes, I know it's difficult to describe, barely put together, blurred and vague, yes, but what's key is that this specialized infantry soldier C, a member of B-3 OP-17, trained me in target practice.

Time passed. If it continued to pass, fall would come and Billie would be fully twelve years old. She expected to turn twelve a few weeks after school began. In the middle of gardening she deliberated over whether Rafael would teach her himself when the time came; perhaps he would send her to boarding school, but she didn't think it appropriate to be the first to mention it. It wasn't up to kids to ask when school began. Grown-up folk should tell them: Hi kids, school starts next week.

They were by the fountain. The sun had moved itself remarkably far to the west, in a shorter time than Billie had expected, but she didn't feel like standing up and measuring the length of the shadows with a ruler, just wanted to hang around in one of the white chairs where the grown-up folk had ideally sat when they wanted to be like adults and discuss matters with serious and subtle comments. The grass reached up under the seat of the chair. She stared at the pink canvas shoes. Boy, she could stare at them. For hours at a time. How fine they were. How well they had done over the summer. Gugga-doll was lying in her arms and also staring at the fine pink canvas shoes. The thermos lay in the grass, and so did some plates with pancakes on them. The kitty slept on the pond bank. While the water was temporarily removed from the pond, the goldfish spent its nights and days in a big jug. Rafael, wearing his painting overalls, stood on a stool and scraped the statue of the pissing boy, got it ready for a new coat of paint. They didn't hear the handle on the garden gate lift because the cow lowed conscientiously at the same time, and they heard the creak of leather soles on the ground only as a rustling in the trees. Hardly any weight at all burdened the collective effort of feet and shoes; the mood was light. Perhaps a puppet on its travels, they traveled so quietly. The chickens in their good chicken manner whispered to one another and scattered in an instant, staring at the traveling walker who stopped at the open door and called out a greeting, then looked around at the lot in front of the house. The wind turned the pages of the open coloring book which lay beside the face-down treasury of verse on the pebbledash table. The walker picked the box of colors up from the grass and set it on the table, peered through the window pane of the greenhouse, where inside everything was in bloom, beautifully-colored flowers, fantastic fruit hanging on stalks, heath-green tobacco plants with white flower buds, odd species of cabbage, and two coffee plants. By the greenhouse there was a surprising gravel bed set in the soil under the highest tree. The traveler walked across it and appeared at the back of the house.

*xxxvi.* Billie got up and Rafael stopped scraping the statue. The cat opened its eyes but closed them again and continued dozing in the grass like black pasta in broccoli. The nun smiled and extended her little hand to Rafael. "Good day, sir," she said; she had a cap on her head and wore brown patent leather shoes, a grey woolen habit, and a white collar visible underneath. A belt was pulled taut around her waist and a tasseled fur pouch hung from it; the girl immediately saw that the nun must keep her money, her rosary, her playing cards, and her alarm clock there, and the book of books in a leather binding with a gold zipper. Rafael set the scraper down, dried his palms on his pants leg, and took the nun's hand.

"Good day, young lady," the nun said to Billie.

Billie curtsied: "Good day, nun."

"I've arrived like an angel," the nun added, laughing at her own invention, "in first class. I've traveled many kilometers today in humble shoes. Humble shoes," she corrected herself, "how can shoes be anything but humble since they're under our soles? No, I must have meant arrogant shoes—" the nun laughed. "It happens that I have no provisions, no water, no anything, no baggage, and I wish I had less need to beg, but don't you live well enough that you can give a poor traveler and pacifist delegate of the holy power, which is entirely powerless in all earthly respects, a little bite?"

"It is better to give than to receive," Billie said, looking for the murderous gleam in Rafael's eyes as he took off his white painting overalls and hung them on the fountain boy's head. The girl thought it was enchantingly daring, getting undressed like that in front of a totally strange nun, even though under the overalls he was fully clothed in blue trousers and the farmer's white smock. She jumped up like the cat, ran from the place, and eagerly dawdled after them. At the doorway he held out his hand and said, "Please, go ahead," the way one doesn't usually say "Please, go ahead." He had a crush on her. Indeed, she smiled beautifully.

He invited her to sit at the dining room table while he went into the kitchen to make coffee. Billie lay on the floor and stared at the woman. Then she turned a somersault, stood on her hands, did another somersault, a forward split, a side split, went into first position, second position, third position, forth position, fifth position, did bras ba, rose up onto the tips of her toes and did arabesques. Rafael set the most elegant crockery in the house on the most elegant tray and carried it into the room in an erect, farmer-like waddle. Perhaps the two of them, the nun + the soldier, would marry, have children, grow old— would their children be Billie's siblings? Would the nun be a bad stepmother or a good one? There were two elegant cups on the tray—someone didn't know how to count—and Rafael set them deliberately on the table. There was milk in an elegant pitcher which accompanied the crockery, and a stylish sugar bowl. Billie sat at one end of the table with her hands under her chin. The nun smiled at Rafael, which distracted him; he went back into the kitchen and returned with sugared strawberries in a deep bowl and set it before the nun.

"Please, go ahead, enjoy the fruits of the earth," he said; he created imaginary creases on his thighs the way elegant people do—Billie didn't know whether astronomers and soldiers generally did that, but she had at least seen piano players do so in movies—and he sat down.

"Can I have some, too?" Billie asked, but she didn't get an answer.

The nun pulled off her headgear, unveiling her long hair and her enchanting, curly locks. As though he was looking at gold in a treasure chest, Rafael stared at her hair, captivated.

"It's best if you pour milk over the strawberries," he said, finally, pointing to the milk pitcher.

"The milk is fresh from the cow. He milked her. This morning. You won't ever get a fresher drink. Don't you want to pour coffee into the cups?" the girl asked—she wanted to be a part of things. No one should be left out. It was like having a new doll when no one knew how it would behave. It was a victory feast in the summerhouse of absurdity.

"Hm, yes. Yes, yes. It's time to do so," said Rafael.

Out of a need to cause some discomfort, Billie stared at each spoonful as it disappeared into the nun's mouth, while Rafael, hunched, gazed down into his empty cup. When the nun was done with the strawberries and had set her spoon down in the bowl, he stood up, cleared away the bowl, and came back from the kitchen with a cake slice on a plate.

"That should be enough to tide you over," he said, setting the plate in front of the nun. "You should eat supper with us. It's not long off."

The nun thanked him and ate the cake. Rafael poured coffee into the cups.

"Aren't you planning to smoke?" asked Billie, hoping to disturb his concentration, but he shook his head. The nun said she'd take a smoke if someone offered one, and she smiled.

"Excellent. Give the nun a smoke, mister man."

Rafael passed the cigarette packet down the table.

"Ah, yes, excuse me. I forget to introduce myself. In the cloister, I know everyone by name. I no longer know how to behave with strangers. Not that I displayed exemplary behavior in such respects in my former life, but at least I was never declared insane nor sent to prison. I am called Agnes Elísabet Karmela. It's a long name, but I assure you it'll be easy to remember. The monogram is decisive. A. E. K. Unforgettable, isn't it? Nuns have long names in order to add some variety to the monotony of monastery life." Agnes Elísabet puffed fast, in a disorderly way, on the cigarette and looked around. "The culture here is most comfortable, such beautiful furnishings, neat. My father had a gramophone like this before he bought a CD player. Most recently, he got a computer."

How strange it was to hear a nun mention her father, that a nun was made by people, homemade, came from the world of humans.

"My father also had this type of music player," Rafael said.

"An amusing coincidence," said Billie, "but shouldn't you offer me some coffee?"

She didn't get an answer. That's what it's like to be a kid. Sometimes you're invisible and often you're in the way.

"Would you like me to put something on the music player for you to listen to, Agnes Elísabet?" asked Rafael.

"Yes, wouldn't that be some good, decent fun. I long to listen to a gramophone disc. They have a much better sound," answered Agnes Elísabet, and she stared at Rafael, who went briskly over to the music player and selected a record to put on the turntable. As far as Billie could see, the nun was gazing mostly at his ass. Typical opportunism when it comes to the flesh.

"Can I offer madam a drink?" he asked in different tone than he had ever used to ask a question, at least as far as Billie knew.

The nun smiled from ear to ear.

"That would indeed be excellent, really neat . . ."

She had no further words in her hoard because she was bursting with joy. Billie slid out of her chair and galloped from the room. That was a boring development in what was otherwise interesting company. Music and drinks. She went out to the back of the house, she knew precisely how things were, she was familiar with the grown-ups' ways, she might well expect no supper, but if supper did happen then she would eat like a boor. How do boors eat? They slobber, chew with their mouths open, hold their tongues out with food on them, their eyes wide open, they let the food slide back onto the plate, chew it like cud, slurp, munch, grease their knives with their tongues, and jab their forks in their teeth. Billie set herself up in front of the big living room window. Rafael was facing the garden. The nun was facing away from the garden. It looked like they were talking a blue streak. Billie made faces. Rafael saw but pretended not to. She put her thumbs in her ears and wiggled her fingers and stuck her tongue out. Flipped him the bird. She took herself further down the garden and settled in the hollow where nobody could see you. Before supper was served she saw the people in the living room dancing.

## XXXVii.

"Though I'd very much like to be with you, I can't because I'm a nun. I can't be unfaithful to Jesus nor to his father and mother."

"If I was a soldier I could rape you, sister."

"No, my love, a soldier can't ever set hands on a nun. There is an unwritten law between the commanders of the armies and the Vatican. Some places must remain sacred."

"Who says that a nun is a nun? Mightn't she be a spy in disguise?"

"Certainly, certainly, my love. It's entirely possible. And you could be a war criminal in disguise as a farmer."

"Aren't there whores who sometimes dress up as nuns in the whorehouse?"

"Zounds. Don't talk like that, young man."

"Sister, you aren't much older than me."

"I will never tell you how old I am, my love, even if you offer me a cool million."

"I want you."

"I want you too. That means I have to say extra prayers at services for the next few weeks. That's the most shocking thing I've discovered since I became a nun, that my body should be enticed by a fellow traveler, yes, a stranger, my love. I have forsworn from living the kind of love life the general public does, and you know what, my love, despite the best efforts of my friends at the time of my decision, I am settled. Abstinence from sex cures you of depression. I have never felt better since I . . . you know what I'm talking about, my love."

"Agnes Elísabet, Agnes Elísabet Karmela, it's like we've known each other always, sister."

"I feel that way too. Perhaps in a former life."

"Can nuns believe in reincarnation?"

"No. But when I am not being told what to believe, I believe whatever I want."

"I like the spirit, nanny baby."

"Kiss me, farmer. One kiss and it's done and we'll forget it ever happened."

"I will, sister. I'll kiss you joyfully and lustfully."

"That was a wonderful kiss, my love. Wasn't it for you, too, my dear man?"

"Yes, the best."

"Now I've betrayed God, Jesus, and Mary, my bonds of duty. Kiss me again, dear man."

"You are the bride of my life."

"I am the bride of heaven. Kiss me again, my dear man."

## xxxviii.

"My love, may I play you a wild wild wild and tragic song which my fellow sister-in-faith, the abbotess, composed fourteen days before she committed suicide?"

"Can nuns commit suicide?"

"Nuns can do everything. May I play it for you, my love?"

"Why did she commit suicide?"

"My love, why does the sun shine? Do you know the answer?"

"Because otherwise nothing would live."

"It's surely good to commit suicide when one has given up on getting any attention. Pass me the guitar, my love. Is it all the same to you if I am naked when I play? I love being naked with a guitar in my arms. It feels so good to play naked. The best thing I know. But you aren't allowed to take off your clothes. Those who are listening can't be stark naked. Only those who are playing. I haven't taken off these nun's clothes since I became a nun, except alone, without anyone seeing. And I could hardly complain about camera surveillance in the cloister. Don't stare at me even though I'm naked."

"I won't stare at you, sister."

"When one stumbles upon and enters a farmhouse, one also wants to be naked, like the animals. This is a neat guitar. My love, do you own this guitar?"

"I wish I did, because then I would give it to you but, alas."

"I would hardly be able to accept it, all the same. The song of the abbotess from fourteen days before she committed suicide."

"Fourteen days?"

"Fourteen days. Listen hard to what she had to say to us fellow travelers, because no one listened until after she was dead. The song of the abbotess."

Hey, wether, do you think you're good, so good
That you don't need to hide in wolfskin
Do you know that you are like us all
On the way to slaughter
On the way to slaughter
On the way to slaughter
Little sweet lamb of mine, o baby yeah—

Knowing too much brings you closer
To the coffin's soft corduroy—blood red pillow
Knowing a little sends you to the nuthouse—o, baby yeah
Perhaps it's better
Perhaps it's better
Perhaps it's better
There than here, o, baby, juicy juicy juicy, fuck it, right on,
        yeah—

Wipe out half of all I know

So I can join in—or I'm stuck on the outside

It's necessary to conceal the conclusion

It's necessary to conceal the conclusion

Or I'm stuck alone on a raft

Alone on a raft

A wounded, grumpy scarecrow, oooo, yeeeeeeah—


To kiss a guy, to toil at a love life

I feel like a retarded kid

Bored by the city's subway system

Red and blue lines, yeah

Soft and good

Calm and polite

Juicy and sentimental—kiss kiss

Red and blue lines, fuck it baby, fuck it, yeah—


Human life is a parody of human life as it used to be

Which was a parody of human life as it used to be

Aided by rebellion, abetted by forgetfulness

Nothing is genuine, baby

Nothing is genuine, baby

Only diamonds are sacred, baby

Diamonds shine more real than your eyes


O baby, take me—N O T

I am lost forever forever forever

O baby, fuck it, right on, yeah

Agnes Elísabet played hard and frantic on the guitar and ended with a strummed flourish. A real power chord in the final bars. Then she said: "My dear and good man, that's how it was." Rafael clapped his palms together: "Depression at its height, depression totally at its height, baby." They kissed.

**XXXIX.** Rafael was standing at the kitchen stove frying eggs when Billie came down with sleep in her eyes. There were beer cans, empty whisky and shot tumblers, dirty glasses and cups, and full ashtrays in the living room. Records and record sleeves lay strewn about the floor. The Barbie dolls and paper dolls were on the rocking chair. The guitar was on the table. The checked guitar case was under the sofa. Billie asked Rafael about Agnes Elísabet. She'd gone. Where did she go? To the city. "Did you kill her?"

"No."

"You swear?"

"Two fingers raised to God."

She couldn't see blood anywhere inside the house, and the house didn't smell like he had been doing any scrubbing. He'd managed to strangle her, then. Billie slipped her feet into her pink canvas shoes, went out, and walked a circle around the house in her nightdress. The sky was ominous but lusty. Big, rain-threatening clouds put on airs, calm and haughty in equal amounts. Storms and rain awaited their cue. Billie escaped inside at once. Rafael put the coffee flask and two plates with fried eggs on the table. She rushed into the room and discovered the sofa was crumpled; she examined it closely. "Why do you think I would have killed the nun?" asked Rafael, his face appearing at the window in the wall between the kitchen and living room. She pointed to the Barbie dolls on the rocking chair:

"Were you trying to be friendly to the nun with these, showing her the Barbies and paper dolls so she would know you were a good guy?"

"Kinda."

"Sentimental."

"Come and eat, windbag," he said, and she sat beside him at the kitchen table.

"Do you have a headache?"

"Not a trace."

"Because you got laid last night?"

"Sssh, zounds," he said, "listen to the mouth on you, child."

"Did the nun teach you to say zounds?"

"No, I've always known it. Stop bickering and eat your food."

Billie shifted neither hide nor hair but sat with the comforter wrapped around her on the rocking chair while Rafael tidied. The rain ran down the huge living room window and sprayed from the clouds down into the pond, on the painting overalls which hung from the neck of the peeing boy, on the Barbie doll Gugga and on the cow, the grave, the vegetable garden. It rang down on the glass-roofed greenhouse, ran the length of the leaves and trees, plink plink plink into the rubber boots on the sidewalk's stone slabs beside the greenhouse, twisted in spirals along the ornate roses in front of the French windows like a worm cut into little linked trailers of drips. Rafael picked up the gramophone discs, as the nun had called them, found the matching record sleeves for the proper records, gathered the albums together and arranged them in the record stack. Put the empties, as Abraham called empty beer cans and liquor bottles, in the black bag. The dirty glasses and cups went in to the dishwasher. He vacuumed, and Billie sat immovable in the rocking chair while he vacuumed around it. He scrubbed the floors. She was still immovable as he moved the rocking chair as well as he could manage. Clever of him to vacuum, scrub the floors, and tidy up while it's raining. The wind sweeps and vacuums. The rain washes. The wind dries and airs. It wasn't any more complicated than that. Fall strolls into the freezer with summer then spring fetches summer back from the cold. The sun is an excellent oven and a good chandelier. The moon a flashlight. In winter, everything stiffens like in a game of statues. In spring, stiff joints begin to creak and then everything starts moving, and on good days each detail dances with every other detail in creation. Now it was time for the cleaning dance. Were the wind and the rain regretting something?

**XXX.** "Was the nun entertaining?"
"Nuns are entertaining because they are free, like Marius."

"Marius was not entertaining, even though he was good."

"But nuns, at least, are entertaining because they don't bother with small talk."

"Perhaps she was a spy, or an emissary from the Tax Office?"

"Then I would be in trouble."

"Was she definitely a woman?"

"Yes."

"How do you know?"

"I just know."

"Did you kiss her?"

"She is a woman. I can vouch for that, darling girl."

"That's the first time you've called me darling girl. Did the nun teach you to say darling girl?"

"No, obviously not. I know many, many words even though I am a soldier."

"When is she coming back?"

"She isn't coming back."

"How do you know?"

"She said: I hope you have a good life forever and ever, my dear sir. If we meet again, it'll be a chance in a million."

"She said that?

"Yes"

"Oof. Tough."

"She has business affairs in the city. Buying a computer."

"You talk differently now that she's gone. Did she kiss some new words into you?"

"One must make use of language, Billie. There are many hundreds of thousands of words in it. Although we tend to like going about in the same clothes, it's also good to change them."

"Don't go making excuses."

"I am not making excuses."

"Did she have a raincoat?"

"No, I don't think so."

"Did you offer to drive her?

"Indeed, she refused the offer. She isn't allowed to travel in cars. She has been commanded to go on foot for all of her travels. Those are higher orders."

"Orders from the other side?"

"She does so as a punishment for violations she didn't want to discuss. And there's not much gas in the car, remember. I would have been promising more than I could deliver."

"You shouldn't be stingy to your true love."

"Agnes Elísabet is not my love, Billie."

"Yeah right."

"No. I am a soldier. She is a nun. I am a former soldier. She is currently nun and betrothed for eternity to the Holy Trinity."

"Is she planning to carry the computer the whole way back? On foot? Let's say it rains constantly. Constantly constantly constantly from now on. There could be a flood. And she doesn't have any boots. Nor a raincoat because she didn't have any luggage, remember, no luggage."

"Perhaps she's allowed to mail the computer."

"Then why didn't she order the computer by phone?"

"Perhaps she needs to take some money out of the bank."

"Why wouldn't she come back the same way, stop in for coffee and drinks, pancakes and a few kisses?"

"She took a detour when she saw the beautiful valley. I can understand that. This is one of the most beautiful valleys in the world."

"I think you've let yourself be deceived."

"No, Billie, if a man plans to stop killing, then he must learn to trust people."

"Did you give her any provisions?"

"Heaps of provisions."

"What did you give her?"

"Hard-boiled eggs, tomatoes, carrots, cabbage, rye bread."

"Were you both mournful when you said goodbye?"

"No."

"How were you?"

"Rather quiet."

"Did you kiss?"

"Yes. The way people do when they say goodbye."

"Did you cry?"

"Actually I did, a little."

"Do you mean that?"

"Yes, Billie. It's been a long time since I've cried. I feel like I've met my soulmate."

"And I? Am I like your soulmate?"

"I don't know."

"What am I like?"

"I don't know."

"Did she ask you about me, about who I was? Did she ask whether I was your daughter?"

"She asked whether I was your brother."

"And what did you say?"

"Yes, that I was your brother. Then she asked me countless questions which I couldn't answer without giving myself away."

"Why didn't you tell her the truth?"

"Then I would have had to kill her. You don't kill nuns. I could never justify that before a court of law, let alone myself."

"Why don't you try to tell the truth to those around you and then not kill people?"

"Perhaps."

"If you meet her again?"

"Then I'll tell her the truth."

"You promise?"

"Yes."

"Why didn't you rape her?"

"Don't behave like that, child."

"How's your head?"

"Neat and good."

"Did the nun teach you to say 'neat'?"

"Stop it, Billie."

"Are you so n e a t and good in the head because she let you go up inside her?"

"What a choice of words, kid. Behave yourself."

"Did you spend the time praying?"

"I will get a headache if you keep on like this."

Billie started to cry. Rafael took her in his arms and sat with her on the sofa.

"There, there, my big girl."

"I am not big."

"There, there, little girl-child mine all sad."

"Did you take a shower this morning?"

"Mhm."

"You didn't take a shower yesterday morning. Why did you shower this morning?"

"I shower when I've been drinking liquor and smoking heaps of smokes."

"You also shower when you've been killing, remember."

"Billie, I didn't kill the nun, I promise."

"Not when you were tipsy?"

"No."

"Or when blacked out?"

Fatigued by his considerable memory, Abraham spent long spells of time in blackouts. Her mom once blacked out when she was camping with her friends. They were fun, then. Billie's first three years went by in a blackout, and many people end their old age like that. Origins and endings framed by memoryless-ness. Her poor mother and father. Poor them.

"No. I don't get blackouts."

"But you went up inside her?"

Rafael prodded the tip of Billie's nose.

"No, I didn't go up inside her, sugar pig."

"Did she ask you your name?"

"I don't remember. I don't think so. I just don't remember."

"Exactly: no she didn't. She never asked for our names. She just formally introduced herself and never asked our names. Huh, who wouldn't want to know the name of the person they're about to kiss." The girl's tears dried. She squinted her eyes to help herself think better. "That's suspicious. Start the car, skipper."


*xxxi.* Where highway thirteen and the side road from the farmstead meet, there is a choice between two directions, as mentioned earlier. The way to the right branches in two at the bottom of the valley, one way ending in a stub by the water, the second way licking the mountain's roots and ending in a hayfield by the old ruins. From there, there is a pathway along the eastern slopes, a hard-to-make-out trail over some inclines, and then across the pot-holed lawn back home to the farmstead.

The orange car headed left, where the highway lifted south-west, up towards the mouth of the valley and then to the Cease-less Heath, where the sun began to shine. Rafael sat confidently at the steering wheel in a white t-shirt; he'd put on a gold ring with a lion's head before they left. Billie wore the pink baseball cap, the one which had belonged to Marius, and now it was time for sunglasses. "If she's a spy I've got to kill her. According to the army commanders' orders," Rafael said, looking emotionally along the road.

"Perhaps you could arrest her and get important information from her?"

"It's difficult to kill one's love, Billie, and just as difficult to arrest her."

Although Billie had a strange interest in other people's loves, this was too sentimental. How could people who farted on average five hundred times a year be sentimental? She took off the cap, lifted one of her butt cheeks, farted. Her companion didn't hear. She bit into Marius's cap.

If only you weren't so romantic, babe, if you weren't so very primal, my Soffia. Try to be guided by intellect, sophistication. Let others see about adding to the population. Although your body is beautiful and attracts others, that will soon come to an end. Billie's grandma pointed to her huge head in support of her point: What's here is more enduring, lasts a teensy bit longer. We must be practical, must be practical, babe. Every day things change, babe. It's better to trust the head than the body. My Soffia, let reason rule your journey. The man you married is obstructing your journey. Life is short, you'll know that for sure when you're approaching forty. I won't mention the milestone that is fifty. You're squandering time, good daughter. My pretty babe.

I'm not squandering time, Mom, said Soffia, who was dressed in her finery, her hair up, wearing beautiful make-up, as she sat on a chair fit for a king. Billie sat on a soft princess's sofa wearing her best dress, with Gugga the Barbie doll dressed in an identical dress, which Soffia had designed and had a tailor sew on the doll for the tea-party with Billie's grandma.

One doesn't spend time like money. Time isn't money, Mom.

Grandma poured more tea into the cup and smiled at her child's child.

You just squander time, babe. Let's all squander time and have more tea. I'm sorry, grandma's little girl. Grandma sometimes needs to scold your mom. Grandma finds it hard to stop being a mother to your mother. Especially since your mom is so stubborn and crazy when it comes to men.

Her mom sipped tea:

Mom, why are you such a snob?

Being a snob protects one, Soffia, my honey-flower. It's that simple. In this world, one meets both good and evil people. Being a snob protects one from people.

A fascinating philosophy, Mom, very fascinating and admirably justified.

Yes, and experimenting with one's sex life, Soffia babe, you can carry on like that for a while, the way one plays about in high school, but later you must treat life seriously. Ambition. Career. Science. It's true, babe.

Mom, isn't it better to hold off talking about all this while there's a child in the room?

I think it's good for a child to hear what I have to say, my pancake, my honey-flower. It's not possible to live just for sex, like you do, passionate, emotional, partying. You can indulge your sexual desire and horse around in the summer holidays. But then take care of yourself; you know what I mean. My heart of gold. I've told you c o u n t l e s s times. But you don't listen to me and that makes me melancholy. That you have never listened or taken advice from your long-suffering mother. A daughter should listen to her mother, my sugarbowl. It's self-evident. I fought this war before you. Now, now, two or three years in the future, then you'll leave this guy.

That's Billie's father you're talking about, Mom. He's Billie's father, Mom.

Yes, yes. And I am her grandma. I'm allowed to say what I need to say, sugar flower. You'll leave him, and what then? You don't think about the big picture before you act, and thus you get led astray.

Mom, will you please stop talking about it now.

Soffia blew her nose with the blue napkin, which she should have used to wipe her mouth. On a gold-colored plate on the table stood a butter cake with pink icing. A single slice had been cut from it, a slice which no one would eat—never—never never never not at any time. Billie crawled up into her mother's arms.

What will you do with the girl then, Soffia babe? What, my big and clever daughter?

Can we talk about something more interesting, Mom?

Soffia dried her eyes with the napkin, which had a picture of a doe and an angel on it.

And what should we talk about, Soffia? Come up with something entertaining, my honey-blade. Something tremendously entertaining which makes us happy. That's what we need now.

Soffia set Billie down on the floor.

Billie, love, run and fetch your windbreaker. We're going. Perhaps you don't think my daughter is good enough for you because she's the daughter of such a strange bird? Perhaps she's not worthy of your tea party? You can give it to her straight. You don't need to watch what you say around her like you would if she was someone else's daughter.

Listen to you, babe. Do you think I don't love my child's child? Weren't you listening to me, babe?

Billie's grandmother stood up. Her mom sat hunched in the seat like she expected grandmother to beat her.

I only said it to make sure, Mom, so I could push away the doubt.

Come on, Soffia. Let's be friends. Come to my arms, sugar flower.

Billie held her pretty windbreaker in her arms, dressed Gugga in her identical windbreaker, and put a red knitted scarf around the doll's neck. Her grandma and mother fell into each other's arms and cried together.

When Soffia next called on the phone (which no longer knew how to ring), Billie would say:

Mom, is it true that I should have just been a stain on the sheets?

She'd first heard that saying from a kid she didn't know.

No, she wouldn't ask; it was too sad a question for her sensitive, tearful mom.

Billie, nothing is wrong with you. How often do I have to tell you. I'm a doctor, wouldn't I be the first person to know?

Perhaps, Mom, you're keeping what you know about me from yourself? Isn't that called self-deception?

Soffia couldn't bear to hear that, and her eyes flooded with tears:

I haven't been a good mother.

You're the best mom in the world, Mom.

You're saying that to comfort me because you're a sweet and polite girl, but others will need to comfort you in the future, for my sake, o my good God, my heart bursts. How can I make amends for my mistakes?

What mistakes, mother?

Having brought you into this strange world.

What strange world, Mom?

Where one hand works against the other. Terrible details matter more than the big picture.

What terrible details, mother? What terrible details?

Terrible details like who your parents are. Where you are born. Whether one has a lot of savings in the bank.

Mom, I'm glad I was born. I'm glad I was.

My love.

Soffia held her girl tight:

I just wish the world looked as good on the inside as it does on the outside.

Abraham explained Soffia's grief and bouts of weeping to his daughter:

Your mom, sssh, don't tell her I told you this, but your mom, sssh . . . Abraham put his finger to his lips: She gets depressed sometimes. That can be difficult for her companions, but I prize it—if she wasn't depressed, she wouldn't ever have fallen in love with a guy like me.

Now that was the strangest strangest strangest and quite unintelligible explanation Billie had ever heard. If this description was correct, then Billie should thank the depression for her being in the world. For having introduced her to Marius the former ballet dancer, who now was dead, she should thank the depression.

The highway through the Ceaseless Heath entered the Endless Pass and passed through it like a spiral, or a colon.

"Somehow, the more I've thought about it, Billie, over and over and over, the more I trust Agnes Elísabet Karmela one hundred percent. I have turned it around and around here on the heath, pro and contra, for and against, spy, nun, nun, spy, no, no, no, that doesn't fit, Agnes Elísabet Karmela is a good woman.

"From the way you say her name, I can tell you love her," said Billie, raising her voice a little to reach over the noise of the car. "You say her name the same way Marius said Maria's. With awe."

"Is that so? Is that really so, Billie?"

"Say her name, and I'll listen hard and work out whether or not it's so."

"Agnes Elísabet Karmela."

"Yes. Really so."

All at once, Rafael was proud, happy, and smug.

"You ought to tell her you love her and ask for her hand. Such a thing happens only once, maybe twice, in a lifetime," a sentence from Soffia, "and now you've finally found the human being who can free your heart from the spell of being a murderer."

"She is completely different from all the girls I've met. I trust her. I entrust her with my body," said Rafael, holding on to the steering wheel resolutely.

## xxxii.

Rafael pointed at the dashboard: "Billie, remember how I taught you about the speedometer a few days ago, well, this here, see, that's the gas gauge. If the hand is here it shows the gas tank is empty. Here, the tank is full. If the hand points to middle, the tank is half-full. You can work it out for yourself."

"One cannot think about everything," said Billie, nibbling on the cap until her drool dripped down on to the material. She sucked up her saliva.

"You are a good traveling companion, Billie. I've known more than a few traveling companions. They've all been boring. But you're a delightful travel companion. It's even good to be silent with you."

Oof, the soldier was being sentimental again. His stock personal defense mechanism. A defense against the murders.

"Do you think I might be retarded?"

She wanted to drag the debate down to a more comfortable level, but Rafael pointed to the red light which winked on the dashboard and said it was the gas tank warning light. She didn't feel like worrying about military fuel supplies. Other people must be working on that at army headquarters. Again she drooled inadvertently on the cap and sucked her mouthwater back up.

"Two companions and I once went on a long-awaited holiday from our training quarters, on a sightseeing tour to one of the most beautiful churches in the world. It had countless towers that were more than seventy stories high. We went up and down all the towers. We didn't want to use the elevator, or rather didn't need to because soldiers are in good physical condition. It was a great test of our strength while on holiday. The other people who were taking a sightseeing tour around the church that day were surprised to see peaceful soldiers there at the same time. One couple turned their noses up at us. As though we shouldn't be there unless we were discharging our official duties. Perhaps they would have been able to rationalize our presence if we'd been occupying the church that day and pointing our weapons at them. People are strange. As if soldiers can't be on holiday. That's a tremendous misunderstanding on the part of the general public concerning the army's task in society. People think we don't do anything but kill and blow things up. We kill out of an evil necessity, in between attending to other obligations, and then we take a break, go on holiday to study churches and other cultural objects. I'd like to take you to that church—and naturally, we'd use the elevator, Billie."

At the pass's end, after a distance of more than two hundred kilometers, the first sign came to light. It said that the route to the left headed towards the city, nine hundred kilometers further, nine hundred kilometers to the stories there. On the sign was a picture of a steep winding path. Underneath was a steep cliff. They looked back and saw nothing which marked Endless Pass or the heather beyond the pass or the valley beyond the heath. Unmarked, too, was the home of the children in Reindeer Woods. The young Agnes Elísabet Karmela must be an Olympic record holder in hiking if she had put a whole heath and a hellishly long pass behind her, and all in the brief time which had passed since she took her leave of the farm in the early hours of the morning. Tired from a lack of sleep, a little drunk, but with sufficient provisions.

Some road workers had created parking space, room for about one-and-a-half trucks, by the sign. Rafael parked the orange car there; anyone seeing it from below, in Forever Valley, would see how good it looked up on the rock outcrop. Billie and Rafael got out of the car. The valley lay before the travelers—it was known for its church, churchyard, a gas station, a small shop, pig farms, a golf course, and its grassy plain, which covered a ninety-degree segment, with a radius of roughly fifteen kilometers; the rest of the circle was taken up by slopes and the sky. The outlines of a hut and gas tanks were just barely visible; no nun. Billie put the baseball cap on her head and the military-green binoculars to her eyes. Wooden planks had been nailed across the hut's windows and its door was sealed with both tape and a latch. The afternoon sun glittered on a million trillion pieces of glass that were laying in front of the gas station. The gas tanks had also been sealed. No animals, no cars, though a red tractor lay on its side in a hole as high as a man. The golf course was overgrown, but a few triangular flags still fluttered on their poles. Nine hundred kilometers to the stories there. Níuhundrað kílómetrar í næstu sögur. Nuevecientos kilómetros hasta los próximos cuentos. Ni hundrede kilometre til de næste fortællinger. Neuf cents kilometres. Billie handed Rafael the binoculars. "No traces of the nun," she said philosophically, and she jauntily prepared herself for the next stage in the hide-and-seek chase of this love story, "and if she is not a nun, she heard the car and ran to hide. Or she has a commitment phobia—" she had heard her mother use the phrase unsparingly in one of her many conversations. Her mom loved the phone as much as she loved her stethoscope. Perhaps she had a deep need for having something in her earholes. "Or is fastidiously loyal to her promise to God," Billie added.

"Perhaps she went another way, directly over the slope, on some trail we don't know about," said Rafael, moving the binoculars up to his eyes. In the long shadows the cabin cast on the parking lot stood a man with binoculars which were pointed at Rafael's. Doubtlessly he was now looking right into Rafael's eyes. Rafael dropped to the earth and tugged Billie down with him:

"Didn't you see the man?"

"What man? I didn't see a man. What man?"

"The man at the gas station."

Rafael crawled to the car, opened the trunk, and, without ever standing up, came back with a huge cylinder; he pieced together the huge cylinder with another smaller cylinder and then inserted a thick holder inside the barrel. Billie pinned herself to the binoculars, which lay on the ground.

"Rafael, what if that's Agnes Elísabet?"

"Don't you see that's a man? That's not Agnes Elísabet. That's a man."

"She could have changed out of her clothes and cut her hair."

"That's not her, Billie, I know. The physique is all wrong."

"You ought to know that."

"I'll only blow up the gas station. To be safe. The place has already been destroyed, really. I just need to dot the i. To finish what others began."

With a few twists, Rafael screwed the case into the cylinder, aimed the cylinder at the gas station, connected a few leads, and looked through the sight again before firing a rocket from the place. Through the binoculars, Billie saw the man—or the nun—run from the parking lot and disappear behind the hill. She was about to say something when the gas station exploded into the air. Thunder reverberated and the earth shook down and then up, in the same way as a body which has been struck. A black dog ran across the green hayfield, turned in a ring; its tail got caught by a half-fallen part of the fence. There was no sign of the man behind the hill. The gas station was nearly level with the earth. A single column of smoke curled up into the sky like an eyelash. Billie put down the binoculars. Rafael broke the cylinder apart.

"That wasn't difficult," he said.

"Wouldn't it be better to write the nun a letter asking her to marry you and fix it to the signpost?"

Rafael rubbed his palms together the way a man does after having set off an explosion, because of the inexplicable resultant dust.

"Tell her you love her. Ask for her hand and fix the letter to the sign in case she strolls past later."

He propped the cylinder up in the trunk of the car, took off one shoe and one sock, got the gun out of his jacket, and shot off a toe, which smashed to pieces. His facial expression went through a series of tremors. He poured a measure of whisky on the toe and put his sock back on.

"Won't you regret it your whole life if you stop here and don't write her a letter?"

Rafael put on his shoe, denied having a headache when she asked him, looked for something to write with in the glove compartment—Marius always kept some stationery, a writing pad, and a copy of his favorite book there, in case for some reason he wanted to look at it during his trips in the car. But he had never gone further in the car than down to the water. Rafael sat beside Billie on the bare earth and wrote the following letter:

# xxxxiii.

Dear Miss Agnes Elísabet Karmela, will you marry me?

Signed,

Former soldier.

Rafael didn't want to leave his name, in case someone other than Agnes Elísabet came across the letter. That should be enough for now. He said:

"Best to take one step at a time. Hitherto I've always been subject to a fear of commitment and that means you can't go far in an affair, isn't that so?"

Billie read the letter over again and again and ate up every single word. After thinking hard she added her own heartfelt comments:

The undersigned witnesses that the former soldier was shot

by Love's arrow when he met you, who is a child of love.

Signed, B.A.S.

It was fun to write a letter lying on your belly behind a stone, in secret, with the smell of mountain grass in one's nostrils and the afternoon sun on both ears. She peered down into the valley. The smoke had vanished. The dog had freed its tail from the fence; he too had vanished, no trace of a soul, and the slopes' shadows stretched long across the valley. The letter writing had delayed their journey a little, supposing they were hurrying. Didn't they have all the time in the world until the next blitz, which could happen whenever?

The traveling companions fixed an envelope, addressed A.E.K., to the sign which marked Forever Valley and the way to the city, nine hdrd. kilometers, then both got into the car at the same time. As Rafael turned the car around in the parking area and the muscles on his arms twitched like a real warrior in a battle with the wheel, Billie again asked how his head was. "I'm totally fine. Perhaps it's the mountain air." He drove the same way back along Endless Pass. Midway along the heath Billie fell asleep in the passenger seat with the baseball cap in her mouth, and moments later the car died on them.

"All for love," she said when she woke up and heard about the gaslessness. It was now completely dark. Rafael beat his knuckles against the steering wheel and said that love turned men into idiots.

"You won't regret this journey," she said, the way her mom would blab on about things with a colleague on the phone:

One day, everything comes back to bite you.

You'll pay for it in the next life.

That's compensation for love.

The soul's money-laundering always comes to light, you'll see.

You reap what you sow.

Love brings us mountains and leaves the car out of gas.

The truth pays.

We fight for people who cannot protect themselves.

A major shit-storm in shit-storm country.

Rafael got out the car, stormed over to the passenger's door, and pulled the girl out. An awful hullabaloo. She held fast onto her hat, skipped back into the car, and lay in the seat, but then he screamed at her.

"It wasn't me who had a crush on this broad!" Billie shouted back. Oof, so many amazing words, so many more amazing sentences, made by idiot-heads for idiot-heads like her: "I am an idiot-head."

"Get out of the car this instant, pretzel-face."

"Idiot-head."

"Huh?"

"Call me idiot-head, skipper. I'm not a pretzel-face. I'm an idiot-head," she said, opening the glove compartment and getting Gugga the Barbie doll and Marius's favorite book. Then she got out in a leisurely manner. Like a lady in a movie. She stretched herself—gwaaaah—breathed in the freshness of the night, and looked up at the sky.

The stars were beginning to shine. Hi, stars. The body's recently-achieved veil of sleep protected her from the evening breeze, but in order to destroy any sign of the journey around the region by a delegate of the army, the current-and-former soldier (or deserter: no decision had yet been taken about his true identity), Rafael blew up the car with everything inside, except a few egg sandwiches, the military bedspread, his soldier's jacket, himself, and his travel companion, who put her hand over her tired, half-closed eyes. The dark shadows turned the smoke invisible, making the tongues of the flames brighter. Her eyes were full of soot and dust. Walkers, like the nun, they set towards home.

"Did you smell the soles of the nun's shoes?" asked Billie; they'd gone about fifteen minutes when she sat down by the road to sleep. Mmmm, a good bed. An excellent blanket. A comforter made of glittering stars. There was the moon, the night-lamp, the searchlight.

"Huh? What's that, Billie?"

Rafael wrapped the military bedspread around Billie, sat beside her on the road, and ate an egg sandwich. The stars sparkled beams down from the surface of the sky.

"Did you smell the soles of the nun's shoes?" Billie repeated in her sleep.

Rafael put the baseball cap, Marius's favorite book, Gugga the doll, and the rest of the egg sandwiches in his jacket pocket, got to his feet, took the girl in his arms, wrapped her in the blanket, and kept walking.

"Why would I have smelled the soles of the nun's shoes?"

"To see if she really was a walker. Perhaps she'd hidden a moped. Or was on a bicycle," Billie answered in her sleep.

"Hm, you've got a point."

"Perhaps on horseback. Perhaps she came by kite. Or parachute."

You can never know with these nuns.

"Perhaps she was an angel," Rafael added.

One never knows with these nuns, what world they're from, whose emissaries they are.

XXXXiv. Half of the leaves on the trees outside in the garden had yellowed. Rafael stood in the kitchen just after midday and dried tobacco leaves on the green toaster, then ground the dry leaves with a mortar and placed the blend on a whole dried leaf which he then rolled into the shape of an ordinary cigarette. The tobacco supply from the army had run out, the chocolate, the coffee, but there was still toilet paper, dried food, cans, headache medicine, and more besides. In the greenhouse, a plethora of coffee beans sprang from coffee plants, and the tobacco plants stood in full bloom. Rafael bound twine around the rolled leaves to hold them together. Billie sat at the kitchen table in the thickest sweater she had brought with her from home, a red-colored one, on top of a yellow sweater; she had yellow pantyhose that belonged to some other kid under her jeans (it was so interesting to wear pantyhose, one of the most interesting things you could wear), and she was drawing a mermaid playing guitar and sitting beside another mermaid who was breastfeeding a young child.

Billie's feet dangled under the table and her ponytail swung as never before; her hair had grown so long. It had to slow down come winter. Hair cannot behave differently from other things that grow, and she could hardly wait for her birthday, couldn't wait to see whether Rafael would know if she had a birthday even though she hadn't ever told him her date of birth. She had marked a red cross on the day in a little red book which lay in the red plastic hamper and was marked, in gold letters, Calendar/Diary. She would never tell Rafael her birthday unless he asked. One didn't reveal it to grown-ups willy-nilly, just to other kids.

Thirty jars with new jams, reds, blues, and yellows, stood beside the kitchen sink. The record player was on; an old record labeled Inga, Marius' mother, revolved under the needle, excellent music to dance to, tuned loudly, it was blasting away when the garden gate opened. The homestead and the garden were filled in no time by a whole herd of sheep and adolescent lambs. At the garden gate stood the shepherd himself, in all likelihood happy and a bit relieved to be returning to society after a long summer on the slopes and countless detours into the wilderness—he was the worst navigator in the history of shepherding. Without having to be asked, the arm on the record player lifted itself and the turntable under the LP slowed down. Billie cleared a pathway through the bleating mass, which reluctantly made room for her—they were somewhat doubtful about the red-colored sweater—and leapt into Isaac's arms. Rafael stopped at the doorway and stared at the youth who embraced the girl in return and whispered to her so no one heard:

"Who is that at the front door?"

"The new farmer in Reindeer Woods," Billie replied, kissing his cold and bearded cheek. Isaac's skin was rough and he smelled like the wind.

"Where are the others?" he whispered before they reached the doorway; this was a smaller reception than could be expected. He was being greeted only by an unknown man dressed in a white farmer's long shirt, the same kind that had covered Marius' torso the spring morning when they'd said goodbye. But the girl didn't answer. Others would have the chance to later. Isaac set the girl down and shook Rafael's hand before being shown in. Bearded down to his chest with a large duffel on his shoulders on his shoulders, he set his walking staff against the doorframe. Rafael lit the smoke he'd been making. "It's a homemade cigarette," he explained, "everything is homemade here, at our home." He slipped his feet out of his flip flops and, barefoot, set to the task of making coffee, like he was the household cook. Isaac looked at the new farmer's toes, but he was barefoot, too, in sturdy leather sandals. Neither was likely to be threatened by a barefoot man. Barefoot men are generally pacifists.

"Take a seat, shepherd," said Rafael, seemingly in good spirits.

Isaac picked up the guitar which stood against the wall and sat down at the kitchen table with the instrument. His fingers searched for the first chord. Rafael set two cups, milk glasses, and some cake and biscuits on the table. But the men avoided looking each other in the eye as they drank coffee; Billie stared at them, unable to make out the exact mood, like when the nun and the soldier sat opposite each other at the dining room table that other time. Could it be love, hate, dread, mistrust, anger, emptiness? One of them was wiry and bent, dressed in threadbare clothes, like a vagabond, the guitar gripped in his arms. The other robust, supple, with sophisticated movements. Billie hiccupped and inadvertently spilled milk from her glass. Rafael got to his feet. Isaac's eyes followed his movements. Rafael wiped and dried the table and sat back down.

"Can I have some more milk?" she asked.

"Hm."

Rafael poured more milk into the glass, filled his cup again with coffee, and Isaac put the guitar away. Billie began to mumble something about the lambs, trying out the art of conversation. The situation gave her a good chance to show off her skills—she was the so-called "link" at the party. She knew both men but neither knew the other. Things depended on her playing her part well. She had never known that there were so many sheep in the world, she said, had there been that many sheep in spring or had she forgotten so quickly? Isaac said that more than a few times that summer he'd run into mistreated lambs, thanks to the war, and he'd added them to the herd, so that they wouldn't be out when winter arrived. It had been a long, warm summer, and if he was in it for the money, he could easily make a profit on the unfamiliar sheep—but he was not in it for the money, he said, stressing particular words, the way people do when their words hide an important political message for their listeners. "One shouldn't profit from others' losses," he concluded.

Rafael nodded his head in agreement.

"One shouldn't profit from others' losses," he repeated. A beautiful sentence which would improve his collection of sentences.

The best thing about it was that the lost livestock had now reached shelter, and thus his mission was done. "Aren't the sheep-houses ready?" he asked Rafael, who nodded his head.

"Yes, of course, more than ready."

"And the barn full of hay for the winter?" he asked next.

"Yes, yes, a great amount."

Then they fell silent, and Billie continued attending to her party duties. Soffia would be thoroughly pleased with her daughter, initiating these conversations, sitting down to eat with two remarkable cavaliers.

"You have such a wonderful haircut, Isaac," said Billie.

The head was cropped short, the beard long and wild and with little curls like a poet's. Isaac laughed heartily.

"I take my barber's tools wherever I go. When the lambs are eating their fill of mountain grass, I've got nothing better to do than experiment with my hair, using the smooth surface of a stream as a mirror. Perhaps a man most spruces himself up for sheep. I am such a clown when I'm alone with them. I get so serious around people. But more of a clown alone with the animals. Thanks, Billie, it's nice to hear a compliment about my haircut."

"Mmm, soft," she said, stroking his beard. It was unlike other beards she'd touched—it wasn't prickly. She thought Rafael might become jealous of the beard and she told Rafael his beard would also be soft when he allowed it to grow.

"Can I see your barber's tools?" Rafael asked, and Isaac dug deep in his duffel.

He had a set of professional hair clippers rolled in a leather pouch that had several compartments, and he kept the scissors and guide combs in the compartments.

"Interesting," he said, studying it closely; Isaac asked if he could use the phone. He was enrolled at the university. He should let them know where he was. That he was on the way to the city at once, that he had brought the sheep back to the house but returning them to the sheep-houses would take at most three hours. Then he'd have to hurry away, he didn't have time to stay the night this time. His studies couldn't wait any longer. It would be fun to see how his classmates reacted to his new haircut.

"Please, go ahead," Rafael answered, "but unfortunately we can't drive you across the heath—the car was hit by a bomb. And in order to pay your wages, we'll need to blow up the strongbox. It would be best if I did that right away, wouldn't it? Shouldn't we get down to business? Shouldn't the shepherd get his money? To buy textbooks and that sort of thing."

Isaac got up from the table and headed towards the phone.

Now Billie wished the nun were here. That the nun and the soldier had gotten married. That the nun was pregnant. Reaching her due date. That they were both smoking pipes as Isaac strolled over to the phone. Perhaps their child would be her sibling, and perhaps it wouldn't change anything if the nun were here.

"Billie, my good girl, go and lock yourself in the hen house," Rafael suggested. Isaac stood beside the phone in the entryway, just about to pick up the receiver, as Rafael scrutinized the hair clippers.

"What about all the sheep and lambs?" she whispered.

"Quickly. Listen up," said Rafael, sticking the leather pouch in his back pocket as he got up from the table. He pulled on Isaac, who was standing at the phone, his telephone call cut off.

"Come on, help me blow up the strongbox, friend. You deserve to get paid for your well-done work." They went into the office with the writing table, the financial papers, the strongbox, and the French windows, on the other side of which the roses were on show in the rose bed, still at their most beautiful, those roses which had formed a romantic background for a portrait photograph. Jenny had arranged the group inside one morning, in front of the window, had set the timer on her camera, run over to join them, and shouted: Smile, everyone! Everyone smiled. The camera quivered until the button went down then up. The photograph was fixed on the film inside the forgotten camera like an embryo which never made it to the round-up with the rest of the herd. As Billie stood by the front door and hesitated, like she was debating whether or not she needed to go to the toilet, she heard the low thud of an explosion. She went over and saw that Rafael was handing Isaac a few bundles of notes, brushing the explosive dust off them. "You earned a bonus, for your energy, Please, go ahead. You could take a girl out for dinner. On me. Isn't that fair, isn't that fair?" Rafael was about to put the bundles of notes down into Isaac's duffel himself.

"You can't buy me, that doesn't buy me," said Isaac. "I don't need anything more than the previously agreed payment. I insist . . ."

"You aren't profiting from other's losses, you're getting what you deserve, my friend. After all that toil rescuing other people's sheep and lambs, think about it. What would have become of the pretty flock if you hadn't put them to use? The world needs people like you."

Then Rafael bent down into the strongbox, and from the hall Billie could see his ass sticking up in the air. Billie frequently got embarrassed if she saw an ass sticking up in the air and felt quite sure she should look away. Oh boy. In front of Isaac. Squash the head in the strongbox. She heard Rafael say:

"Remarkable, I think I've found a book here."

"Only Billie is allowed to touch that," said Isaac, and blood rushed to the girl's head. Her heart struck fast and she stiffened up. What could she alone touch, the girl with the agitated heartbeat? She could barely catch her breath. This must be what a racing car would experience if you pushed the gas and the brake and turned the steering wheel all at once. Opposing forces pulled on her body. The silence, concealing her. The need to make her presence known with a noise. Shy, ashamed of this attention that was falling unreservedly down upon her alone. Only-Billie-is-allowed-to-touch. What was only hers?

"The Book of Laws, by Abraham, Billie's father, a puppet and amateur jurist." She heard Rafael rattle it off as though reading aloud from a sheet of paper. The girl recognized the style. "I dedicate this book to my daughter Billie Abrahamsdaughter and hope that what is written here will never be read by anyone but her. With deepest respect, your father. This book belongs to Billie," said Rafael, but Billie ran outside, burning hot blood rushing inside her, and zigzagged through the herd of sheep which made way for her, her red-colored sweater visibly alarming to them, she ran out to the greenhouse and grabbed the vacuum cleaner. It was only ever used outside the house. In the greenhouse, the garage, and the car, but no one ever seemed to have had the idea of using it to vacuum the hen house. Poor them. Having to do their laying, a tremendous job, in filth. She turned on the ceiling light in the hen house. The chickens all there in their right places; they had fallen back with the arrival of the herd, which filled every square foot of the lot—you could compare them to the crowd at a rock concert in a sports stadium, even though it would be a little bit absurd to do so.

She closed the door and connected the vacuum cleaner to the outlet, which until then had only been used for light bulbs and the electric knife; she pressed the on switch. A vertical line in a circle. An unbearable sound from just one machine, but there was nothing to be done about that. That's just how it is. Vacuum cleaners take up a great deal of space in one's ears, but they also have to fill themselves full of unwanted junk and then keep it stored inside. She pressed the switch again; this time it was the off switch. One needs to preface one's activities. The vacuum fell silent. The girl cleared her throat:

"Good day, little chickens. I am the spring-man. I suppose I should vacuum in here. Today's Saturday, and that's when people clean their residences and also the hen houses, though less frequently since animal-kind has fewer requirements. Perhaps because nature is expected to see to cleaning itself. But how are you going to get swept? God's natural brush, storms, never reach in here, do they? Poor you. In your shitty beds. But I still envy you. A little. Not much. A little."

She pressed the on switch and vacuumed the chickens coop. That was a big, necessary task which might have been thought of long ago. Then she pressed the off switch. How inspiring when one and the same thing has two names for opposing characteristics. As if she was Soffia's daughter on every second day and Abraham's on the others. Soffia's daughter from twelve midnight to twelve noon, and Abraham's daughter from twelve noon until twelve midnight. Or vice versa. Offonswitch. Abraham's daughter and Soffia's daughter. Soffia's daughter and Abraham's, Abraham's daughter and Soffia's. She yanked the vacuum cleaner from the outlet and lay down, as it's good to do if you have been busy cleaning. At least, that's what her mother and father tended to do on Saturdays, before they took a bath, because you only did that on Saturdays, cleaned yourself after you'd cleaned up around you. Good to break up the washing with a chicken-snooze, and Billie took a chicken-snooze. A cozy bleating from outside kept her company, the thick air inside saturated with down, with chicken shit, with eggs, the laws of nature at work, incessant production. Two little chickens lay down beside the crook of her neck and slept there. Another chicken stood sentry at her feet in their pink canvas shoes, staring constantly at the girl as she slept.

The earth boomed under the hundreds of feet of sheep and half-adolescent lambs, but when Billie woke the sounds in the world had radically changed. She peeped out through a narrow crack in the door. There was nothing to be seen in the farmstead or in the yard in front of the house, but in the corner by the pebbledash table, directly opposite the shrubs on the other side of the old shelter wall where they had sometimes sat and read, where she often went with her doll tea-party, books, and playing cards, there lay twenty fallen sheep and another twenty lambs. Rafael was standing over the carcasses, supporting one hand on an axe and blowing tobacco smoke. He was wearing the blue turtleneck sweater with an orange cap on his head. On the other side of the enclosure, further down the valley, went the now-wild herd. The bleating moved further off. The air was cool and Billie had not brought her windbreaker from home with her, just a raincoat and a denim jacket, but you often get a windbreaker as a birthday gift if your birthday is in fall. She crawled out of the hen house. She continued across the hayfield on all fours and lay at Rafael's feet, right next to his mirror-shiny military boots. He threw the cigarette away and took the girl in arms. "I am a farmer who can't slaughter animals. I don't know anything about how to go about this, how to work the slaughtered animals before winter, how to skin the animals."

Billie looked over the food-remainders before snuggling up to the crook of his neck and closing her eyes—she wasn't entirely awake. Darling girl. These days a chick. How would Maria feel without the smell of Marius?

"If someone comes to visit, Billie, from now on, would you agree to be recognized as my wife?" Rafael asked, stroking her long hair, which had gotten matted from doing the cleaning and napping on the floor of the coop.

She didn't think about it very long: "Perhaps it's better to be your daughter or sister?"

"No, I don't want to be thought of as your father or brother. That's too sacred."

Either the game would be entertaining or it would be over-whelming.

"But if a man takes a woman, don't they make a marriage contract?" asked the owner of the book of laws, for although she wasn't meant to know the book had been discovered in the strongbox, she wanted to subtly move the conversation in that direction. "And in addition to his signature, the best man should be present and should write below the contract as a witness." She knew that much about marriage. Rafael made a move to put Billie down, like a rejected man who lets himself be in a bad mood for no good reason. "The chickens, the cat, the cow, and the ducks can write below," she hurried to say, holding onto the man.

"Would you be my wife if we held a ceremony as a couple with the animals and ducks as the best men?" he asked, looking her in the eye.

"We'll let the hens sign the contract," she said, adding, "and stamp the cat's paw in the ink," but she didn't want to sound like an over-zealous bride who beams ear to ear with unbridled joy in her happy high. Her body refused to be that kind of bride.

They headed home to the house. But she didn't step foot through the doorway, she waited outside while Rafael tidied up. She didn't want to let him carry her across the threshold, the way he was planning to once he finished the cleaning and tidying. She let him pull her inside and hand over her dowry in her parents' absence:

The Book of Laws, by Abraham, Billie's father,
a puppet and amateur jurist

He said something about how he had found it in the strongbox, that it was best she get the book at once. Billie handled the work, ran it under her nostrils and smelled it; she inhaled the scent of oranges, tobacco, her father's beard. They sat side-by-side at the dining room table; until now they'd never sat at the table without sitting opposite each other. She opened the book of laws, which began with a few prefatory words:

Life is a golden opportunity for each person born into it.

**XXXXV.** Billie turned to the table of contents: About birth. About childhood and youth. About feelings. About finances. About old age. About violent moods. About temperance. About comprehension. About incomprehension. About crime. About murder. About the difference between right and wrong. About property and ownership. About teeth. About the need to listen for cognitive activity. About each person's duty and devotion to their body. More generally about devotion. About union. About divorce. About telecommunications. About matters of religion. About illness and accidents. About journeys. About absence. About marriage in the broad sense. About marriage in the narrow sense. About the marriage ceremony. There it was. She turned to page seventeen.

"For me, it's a real honor to be Abraham's son-in-law, even though it's nothing but make-believe," said Rafael. "A necessary step which has to happen for life in Reindeer Woods to continue to thrive. A man who gave himself over to this and bequeathed his daughter a thick hand-written book."

Oof, her future husband had fallen into a pit of sentimentality. That said, this boded well, though then again he didn't have many left to kill other than the bride, the hens, the cat, and the cow—and there was little danger of this given that they were not dead yet.

Page seventeen:

About marriage in the broad sense. It's good to love another person, but neither love nor a sex life are necessary prerequisites for marriage. Even so, as things stand it's forbidden for close relatives to enter into marriage. The ancient rural community defines the marriage as the region where sex life forms, basically, a definite unity, just as the earth inside an enclosure is the farmer's holding, in which animal and plant husbandry get cultivated thanks to human interventions. Marriage is an accord in which two people (and, in the future, even more than two, when marriage is defined in new ways) agree to establish a home together. By an equivalent agreement one, two, or more enter into a business merger, but instead of working at a business location with the needs of the market as the guiding light, you work at home with the needs of the body and people as the guiding light. Each and every person creates a need for themselves in this life, so evidently a loss results, temporarily, after their death or some other kind of absence. And thus the parties to a marriage create a need for each other, and so a gap (an emptiness) forms (temporarily) with their passing or some other kind of absence. That is the purpose of marriage. The priest creates a need for himself, although in reality there's no need for a man like him. But in order to make ends meet, to provide for himself, he arranges it so that he's a necessary figure in a marriage ceremony. An eyewitness on behalf of humankind and the power beyond humankind.

"How interesting," said Rafael formally, but Billie didn't feel like reading any more or dedicating her time to this game now, and she slipped off the seat, intending to crawl under the table and away, but Rafael grabbed her by the nape of the neck:

"Have you decided not to marry me?" he asked.

"No, no, you don't stop getting married to someone just because you get out of your chair."

"I want to go through with this. I won't go to sleep unless I'm a husband. I won't risk the chance of someone coming here. Someone is always coming here unexpectedly."

The bridegroom stood up.

## *XXXXVI.*

They arranged the Barbie dolls on the writing table in the room with the ruins of the strongbox, the financial papers, and the French windows. It would be called sitting in the front pew if the dolls were in church. Ragga and Sara whispered together how amazing it was that a little girl was getting married but then kids today are more mature than before and different laws apply out in the country. Children are valued participants in country life. They are not the same chocolate donuts and idle consumers as children in urban society are nowadays. Those prissy pampered pigs. In the country, children are proper pigs. Then they didn't feel like talking about it anymore, who does?, they yawned in chorus, the difference between the proper pigs and the pampered pigs was all of a piece. Beside them sat Gugga and Teddy. Gugga had a noose around her neck—she had tried to hang herself earlier in the month. The paper dolls sat on the next bench. They were either naked or in paper-doll clothes. It was difficult to get the cat to stay in its place. "Kitty, stay here, we folk are getting married." The girl sneezed. Rafael set the milk bowl by the foot of the writing table, and that kept the cat in place. They fetched some chickens and let them into the room.

Billie arranged the kitchen stool in front of the French windows. A romantic background. Then she ran upstairs to the bedroom and dressed herself in a floor-length nightdress and put on her rabbit-head slippers. She combed her hair lock by lock in front of the kid's mirror inside the upstairs bathroom, getting rid of the tangles. She had seen young brides in movies combing their hair in front of the mirror. Spegil, spejl, espejo. She put on some yellow earrings.

Rafael got dressed in his military uniform, shouldered the machine gun, and positioned himself in front of the French windows.

The fine chandelier on the ceiling was switched on. It had been inherited from Marius's father; he had resurfaced it right before he died, so that someone could now get married under his chandelier in a remote valley, in an old country farm, a few years later.

Billie clambered up onto the kitchen stool. The soldier offered her a helping hand. That moment, when he took her hand to help her climb onto the stool, caused her to briefly accept her role in the game; until then, deep down she had grumbled about every-thing. But she had also heard Soffia's male and female friends saying that most people suffered astonishingly at their marriage ceremonies. Some got one-hunded-and-four-degree fevers. Some vomited both before and after. Some wept and wept like they didn't want to get married, when in fact they fervently wanted to. Some fainted. Some had epileptic fits, though they'd never ever had an epileptic fit before, and they became epileptics from then on. Soffia and Abraham had not gotten married. I would marry you, Soffia said to Abraham, if I were uneasy about things, but I am not uneasy, so then why do I need to marry you? One gets married if one has weak nerves, in order to calm those nerves, Abraham. Instead, they celebrated Vanity's birthday, the fourteenth of January each year, since love amounted to vanity. Rafael was probably weak-nerved. Therefore there was a motivation, a premise: a current inner turmoil. He brought Billie the book of laws. Billie read aloud from the prefatory words:

> Life is a golden opportunity for each person born into it. To live involves going upright like a soldier and humble and bent-shouldered like a farmer towards life's goal line, your hands full of invisible gold.

She shut the book again and threw it down on the floor; she didn't feel like reading any more. Who thought that a girl like Billie felt like reading any more about the gold which glows and the gold which doesn't glow and the sun's gold and life's golden opportunity?

"With this, I declare that Billie and Rafael are married in the face of God and mankind," she said, and Rafael both saluted and took leave of his military ways. The chickens turned to face the other way; they understood better than the dolls and the paper dolls that the ceremony was over, and they went towards the closed door that opened on its own, like in a ghost movie.

The bride and groom arranged themselves for an invisible photographer. He used a flash because the shadows were drawing in; hopefully the flash wouldn't reflect off the windowpane and the roses behind it would still appear in the background.

Rafael fished a black book out of his breast pocket and also a pen, the same color. On each of the two his name and *ubi bene, ubi patria* was written in gold letters. He opened the book and handed Billie the pen:

"Would you kindly sign here?" he asked, and Billie wrote her name under the following text:

> The under-signed, Rafael August, member C in infantry division B-3, has agreed to take Billie Abrahamsdaughter in these fall days. The marriage is a mutual union between the two of them, and they agree to join forces to take care of the farm at Reindeer Woods, to see the animals are provided for, to manage the earth. Because of the bride's age they will not conduct themselves like a man and woman in a marriage bed.

"Do you want to stamp the cat's paw here too?"

He didn't want to.

The black book sparked the girl's amazement and soothed the mental turmoil you might, she thought, well call stubbornness. I have a deep-rooted stubbornness when it comes to my Abraham, she'd heard Soffia say. Why do you have a deep-rooted stubbornness? she'd also heard Soffia say, and one day she would say that to someone, too, if not to herself. But she did not feel like asking about it today and especially now, when this black book came between her and her stubbornness and sparked her wanderlust, her yearning and curiosity. Hopefully she would get to flip through the book one day. For now, she carefully picked her father's book off the floor. It was unjust to throw one book down onto the floor then stare with such greedy eyes at another.

"May I?" asked the new husband, pointing at the book of laws. She felt sure it wouldn't be any use if she said, May I, and pointed at the black book; the question could prove dangerous.

The book might even be storing secret war documents and descriptions. Billie handed Rafael her father's book of laws.

"Now Abraham and Marius are my models," he said; he stuck the black book back in his breast pocket, set a course for the living room, and sat in the rocking chair with the deerskin covering.

Billie snatched up her dolls and put them into the red plastic box. The paper dolls, too. She was bored. Yet it was a shame to let herself be bored like this when so many were dead. A very great shame. She was on the verge of kicking her foot into the ground, like an old woman scolding her kids, because it was such a great shame to let herself be bored. What should she do now? Stand on her hands? And so she did that for a little while in the hallway before returning to the living room with the treasury of verse in her hand and lying down on the sofa.

She wouldn't turn to the poem which she sometimes turned to when she was alone, letting it bring tears to her eyes by the time she reached the middle of the third stanza. She would never turn to it in another person's presence. She would only flip through some of the other poems, as you do when you're the wife of a man who reads his father-in-law's book of laws for entertainment. She had seen that before in old movies. A married couple sitting in a room through the evening and reading. Her mom and dad had done that, too. But, boy, how cloying they could be. Then for a time they weren't cloying at all. Or perhaps they were always cloying. Her mom and dad. Sentimental and holy.

The darkness filled the huge living room windows—it had now reached the time of year when darkness comes early of an evening. Billie hid her feet under the colorful crocheted rug. She heard some baa-ing. Baa, baa. A remote baa. Then the cow lowed and came towards her sleeping spot near the house. The cat leapt up into the husband's arms in the rocking chair. Billie put her head on the green cushion and flipped away from the poem she would never read in anyone's presence, and she arranged herself more snugly under the colorful blanket. She had only brought summer clothes to this summer farm camp for the children of urban folk, here in Reindeer Woods, but the thick red sweater came in handy. She'd found a scarf, a cap, and some mittens in the hat basket beside the shoe stand and those yellow stockings in the red closet. Perhaps, as he'd said, Rafael was going to sew her some rabbit-skin gloves and had also thought about sewing her a lambskin coat. That would be husbandly. How would Maria feel without the smell of Marius?

*XXXXVii.* A man wearing sunglasses stands outside the gas station on another planet and turns off the lights in the parking lot. There's one gas tank, it's red, and it carries on being red even though the lights are off. A dog gets to its feet from a dog basket outside and follows the man inside. This gas station doesn't have a restaurant, even though many gas stations do, nor a shop selling maps, flashlights, work gloves, string, sponges, and clamps. The gas here is not for sale, although there is plenty. Inside the hall are two doors, the front door and an inner door that the man opens; the dog follows him in. The light inside this new room is cast by a stout lamp which hangs in the air over a big thick table, and on top of this lies a trunk with many attached parts. A second man, who isn't wearing sunglasses, picks up the left arm from the table and takes it over to the shelves where more arms lie, all of them left arms. Then he takes the right arm and sets it down on another shelf, which is actually full of right arms. One leg he sets on the shelf of left legs, the other leg on the shelf of right legs, the feet on the foot-shelf, left, right, left, right. The trunk itself goes into a chest, but he puts the narrow head into a waste-basket; since no two heads are alike, one can never use the same head twice. The puppet's clothes soak overnight. At dawn, he will take them up and hang them on coat hangers, then leave them to dry outside. The man who just came in with the dog sits in a rocking chair and massages the area around his eyes after taking off the attractive sunglasses, which he wears habitually because he can't see.

Now we've got to send someone else to gather together the laws of nature and the laws of society from planet Earth. It could take us fifty years to get him back, and even then he might come back empty-handed, like this one. Comrade, could we end up waiting forever to gather these legal materials from Earth?

Yes, yes, why not? the other one says, as he tosses the head into the waste-basket and at the same time throws away some blank pages that were inside the puppet.

If only we could send a few at once to do the collecting, a whole army of puppets to do the collecting, pipes up the blind man, but we don't have enough manpower for that. The puppeteers are an impossible mess. Love-sick, alcoholic.

The puppeteers are not an impossible mess, the other man insists. For in the taverns spirited people sit around drinking, and they have all the time in the world to air their wisdom. There is plenty to be gained in jurisprudential terms from sitting in a tavern.

There's such great inconsistency in the Earth-dwellers' thoughts, such a terribly great inconsistency. Perhaps there's no workable way to collect the laws. The blind man shakes his head.

We can't give up. I'm going to throw the head out in the trash immediately. He'll disturb our dreams all night if he's lying in the waste-basket. I'm taking him out to the barrel right now.

Listen, can I take another look at his blank pages?

They're blank and you're blind; they're blank and empty and you're as blind as a post.

The man in the rocking chair massages his eyes some more before once again putting on the sunglasses. The other one hands him the empty pages on his way out with the waste-basket. The blind man sniffs at the pages, holds them up close. They smell of a dental clinic. The head goes out to the trash. The infinitely large gas-barrel in front of the gas station farts, and a belch escapes from the pump as a single drop falls on the pavement, where it glitters at him like a hundred-watt gemstone, its beam visible to all the upside-down heavens. Billie sees it through the living-room window and looks over to where Rafael is reading the writings which the men on the planet don't have in their hands. She is no longer the only owner of the manuscript, the words her father gathered from the planet for his daughter: once you're married you don't own anything by yourself and so what? Nobody owns planet Earth. Who owns the girl? Rafael bursts out laughing. Then he looks up from reading, as though he realizes she's staring at him, and he asks her to listen as he reads aloud from the book of laws:

> There remains one area which the legislator cannot bring under the law—people's wishes. In all likelihood, the authorities are fully conscious of the power and strength of their subjects' wishes and they keep up with them regularly. It's interesting that wishes are very contagious. It's part of the poets' and singers' work to put into words the mute wishes of the people. A great responsibility rests on their shoulders.

Rafael's body wiggles in laughter. "One hundred percent sincere and naïve," he says. Billie bores in her nose a little without him seeing. "Listen to that." He laughs. It's a sweet laugh. "People should be entrusted with their own lives. People must be independent in every respect. No one should own anything. Property should be free like people are. The roads should not belong to any one person, in order to stop someone from collecting tolls from travelers. A priest shouldn't take a toll for prayers. A farmhand shouldn't take a toll for the fruits of the earth. The phone company shouldn't take a toll for conversations. Totally free of charge, like the fetus's time inside the mother continues to be after its birth." Then he looks up from reading into the girl's eyes. "The earnest, and somewhat melancholy, clown, my father-in-law, your dad."

"Do you want to play Barbies?" Billie asks.

"Why not?" replies Rafael, "Good idea," he adds, standing up. As he stands by the bookshelf getting the red plastic box, his body changes from a husband's body and a soldier's to a boy's body. Billie stands up. She hardly feels like playing Barbies. She feels something has changed now she's married. She's not as retarded as before, but she has to go through with the idea, which was hers to begin with, and so they sit on the floor.

"I'll play Gugga, I'll play Sara, you play Teddy and Ragga," Billie orders, and without further ado she throws herself into the game—

Kristín Ómarsdóttir has published books of poetry, short stories, and novels, and written plays for the theatre in her native Iceland. She received Gríman, the Icelandic playwright award, in 2005 for her play *Tell Me Everything*. *Children in Reindeer Woods* is her first novel to be translated into English.

Lytton Smith is a founding member of Blind Tiger Poetry. His book, *The All-Purpose Magical Tent*, was selected by Terrance Hayes for the Nightboat Prize. His poems and reviews have appeared in such publications as *The Atlantic*, *The Believer*, *Boston Review*, and the anthology *All That Mighty Heart: London Poems*.